SCUM AND VILLAINY

CASE FILES ON THE GALAXY'S MOST NOTORIOUS

CODEX 19399Z/433_REP

SCUM AND AND VILLAINY

CASE FILES ON THE GALAXY'S MOST NOTORIOUS

CODEX 19399Z/433_REP

LAW, ORDER, AND FAMILY

BY COMMISSIONER EXANTOR DIVO

SEVENTEEN GENERATIONS OF MY FAMILY HAVE WORN THE badge. We all swore oaths to uphold the law and defend the fabric of society from those who would have it fray. It is a demanding call that requires great responsibility. Through each generation, our family has faced the worst the galaxy has offered. We have born witness to those who threaten the stability of society. As I look back through the assembled evidence, anecdotes, and ephemera from cases my family has supervised or been involved in, it is not only a unique family record, but also an account of the criminal underworld and the notorious individuals who have shaped it.

While the era of the Republic was a time of relative peace, its comfort and complacency allowed the rise of the Clone Wars and the deep entrenchment of criminal activities in the back alleys of the Core and a safe haven in the Outer Rim. It was a time of bounty hunters with morals that can be bought, opportunistic pirates, illegal gambling and racing, and the ever-present threat of the Hutts.

As corruption seeped into the shadows cast by towering authorities, the Galactic Empire gave rise to black markets and the smuggling of illegal spice and other substances. Imperial leaders, who covered up the worst of their totalitarian acts, fostered an era where such acts were mirrored in local law enforcement. The habitual blind eye allowed cartels and crime syndicates such as the Crimson Dawn and the Crymorah to not only strengthen their hold on certain worlds but to expand their influence into once-peaceful worlds. It also bolstered the use and need for hired guns and those who operated on the fringes of the law.

The rise of the Rebellion and the hope it offered to a downtrodden public added new complications. It became harder for the Empire to brand the rebels as terrorists after the dissolution of the Imperial Senate made clear the Emperor's agenda. Local enforcement agencies were subsumed by the Imperial doctrine and treason became the number one crime. After the fall of the Empire, the long, hard process of repairing a galaxy began. It is a world where the new leaders were once branded criminals, and its stance on crime has given rise to even more powerful criminal organizations and violent lawlessness.

As the galaxy turns itself politically inside out every generation, those who would defy the law are a constant, shaping the story of the galaxy in surprising ways. My mother wore the badge during the time of the Galactic Civil War; my grandfather, during the Clone Wars. Today, I try to keep order in a turbulent galaxy under the New Republic. Together my family can trace the seedy battles fought against those driven by greed, fame, survival, and political ideals to live a life of crime. These are our successes, our stalemates, and our failures. Our combined files tell the tales of the galaxy's most notorious criminals.

Exantor Divo

Exantor Divo / POLICE COMMISSIONER

COMMISSIONER EXANTOR DIVO has served as head of law enforcement on Hosnian Prime for the past four years. He has thrice been awarded the New Republic Medal of Distinguished Public Service, and hails from a family whose men and women have devoted their lives to uphold the law. He lives in the capital city with his partner and two children.

Tan Divo
POLICE INSPECTOR

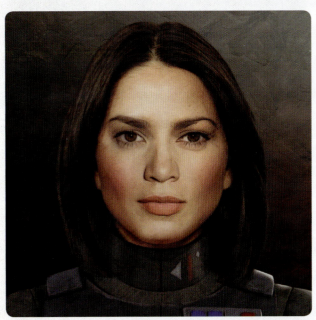

Andressa Divo
IMPERIAL SECURITY BUREAU AGENT

Exantor Divo
POLICE COMMISSIONER

CONTENTS

I

THE LAST DAYS OF THE REPUBLIC

A thousand years of peace breeds a complacency that draws crime like a magnet. That terse observation came from Tan Divo, my grandfather, who was a police inspector in the Federal District of Coruscant. He stated this during a deposition hearing that faulted his police procedures for allowing narcotics from the deeper levels of the city planet into the halls of the Senate. His voice was flat and his words to the point, cutting a jarring contrast to the the puffed-up outrage that colored Senator Aks Moe's questioning.

Grandfather Divo had been a part of law enforcement in the capital since his start as a patrolman after graduating from the police academy. Throughout his career, he championed creating a network of information that would extend to the beat cops operating in the deeper levels of the planet. He knew that only through coordination could they stem the flow of illicit goods from the depths and cut the chain of demand stretching down from the upper levels. His proposals were thwarted at every turn by judges, lobbyists, and other politicians who, on a diagram marking the flow of credits, drew a line directly back to Senator Moe.

This was the state of law enforcement and politics on Coruscant during the twilight years of the Republic. Wistful recollections of this bygone era have a tendency to paint it brightly, and leave out the shadowing of corruption and hypocrisy. The wealthy and powerful repeatedly found ways to remain untouchable, high above the law, protected by money and influence. Petty thievery and street crime were constants, as always, but the real public menace was graft and corporate crime. The criminals with the biggest haul of innocent citizens' hard-earned credits were the barons of trade and industry who bought politicians like collectibles and caused them to work against the interests of their constituents.

Inspector Divo knew the currents he was fighting against to reach justice upstream. By picking at small cases, he hoped to build a larger one against the crime lords that ran free in the capital and the politicians who did business with them. In this time, the vaunted Jedi Knights claimed they were guardians of peace and justice, and indeed they did focus on larger issues of piracy as well as sovereignty and interplanetary disputes. But because their missions were appointed to them by the Senate or, in rare instances, the Supreme Chancellor, it was unlikely they would ever really investigate the problems at home. It seemed like law enforcement on Coruscant was on its own.

The Clone Wars, one might think, would help lower or at least flatten crime rates, as the galaxy focused on the larger questions of survival. Instead, war shortages created new needs, and new black markets to fill. The war also created new bedfellows. To wage war against the Separatists more effectively in the tangle of the Outer Rim Territories, the Republic entered into treaties with the Hutt cartels, effectively legitimizing their operations and opening a gateway for their wares to the Core worlds. Regarding this strategy, no one thought to ask the opinion of local law enforcement.

The war that ended the Republic and the Jedi Knights created a new era in crime. The Clone Wars displaced so many, impoverished billions, and made others wealthy. This imbalance of resources is a feast that crime, the most gluttonous of parasites, feeds upon. It would take decades to recover from the Republic's death, with a false promise of newfound security easing the public into thinking a brighter future lay ahead. Those who had worked the streets and watched the flow of money and illicit goods, as Tan Divo had, knew better.

My grandfather reached out to other worlds to understand how they operated and avoided the pitfalls of such darkening times. He researched racketeering cases and incidents pointing toward larger criminal conspiracies, looking for solutions, and this chapter includes some of his exploration in addition to the direct cases he was involved in. The discovery of his case files, thought lost in the chaos of the Clone Wars, has been a gift to historians not only studying law enforcement, but also tracing the players and the influence they wielded within the criminal underworld. And, if I may, added important chapters in the history of my family.

FILE / 7953.441.3

GRADUATION FEDERAL DISTRICT POLICE ACADEMY CLASS OF '953.4

Tanivos Exantor Divo was born on Level 3215 of Coruscant—far from the sun-lit surface of the capital, but still above the most dangerous levels. In his native Gavas-Eclat neighborhood, urban blight seeped between the lower-class apartments and the reduced-capacity industrial areas. With this blight came parasitic criminals that targeted the hardworking denizens of Gavas-Eclat, shaking them down for what little they had.

This was the backdrop of Divo's childhood. He helplessly watched as his father was forced to part with hard-

earned credits to pay thugs who fed off his fear. It hardened Divo, instilling him with a rigid sense of justice and fairness. Applying himself in his academic study, he earned a scholarship to the Federal District Police Academy at age sixteen.

He graduated valedictorian at FedPoAcad, speaking before that session's roster of 4,500 newly minted deputies, with stirring words, excerpted here.

"We've taken a look at the world around us—Coruscant, whose very

name means glittering—and found it wanting. On a world of luxury, we don't have the luxury to marvel at the heights, or be distracted by the views. We peer into the shadows, so our neighbors don't have to be afraid walking through them to get home. We are deflectors—often invisible, always reliable—warding them from dangers they need never worry about. We look in the shadows not because we see the worst in people—but because we want the best to be safe."

ARREST OF SUSPECT Z. ONGLO

Coruscant is a world of tiers, socially and geographically. Concentric layers of urban overgrowth cover its entire surface, with one age's skyscrapers becoming the thick foundational pillars of the next age's stratum. For millennia it has grown this way, each numbered layer adding a ring like the layers of an ancient tree.

On the lowest levels, the under-world dangers rise. Species tribalism runs deep on Coruscant. Clusters of immi-grant cultures carve out territories of homes and businesses, resisting the benefits that come from more fully integrating with the myriad species found on the capital world. The lower-level police wear all-enveloping uniforms that obscure any defining traits that may identify an officer as belonging to a specific species. The uniform, however, also limits officers' ability to make connections—connections that "face officers" with clear visages are able to forge on the upper levels. That is the price of working the depths.

On this night on Level 1671—3,456 levels from the surface—Zodu Onglo, a Utapaun male, twenty-three standard years of age, was apprehended for aggra-vated assault after a botched attempt to sell a cache of stolen weapons. Further inspection by Lt. Divo uncovered a conn-ection to the Wandering Star criminal syndicate based out of Level 1313.

12

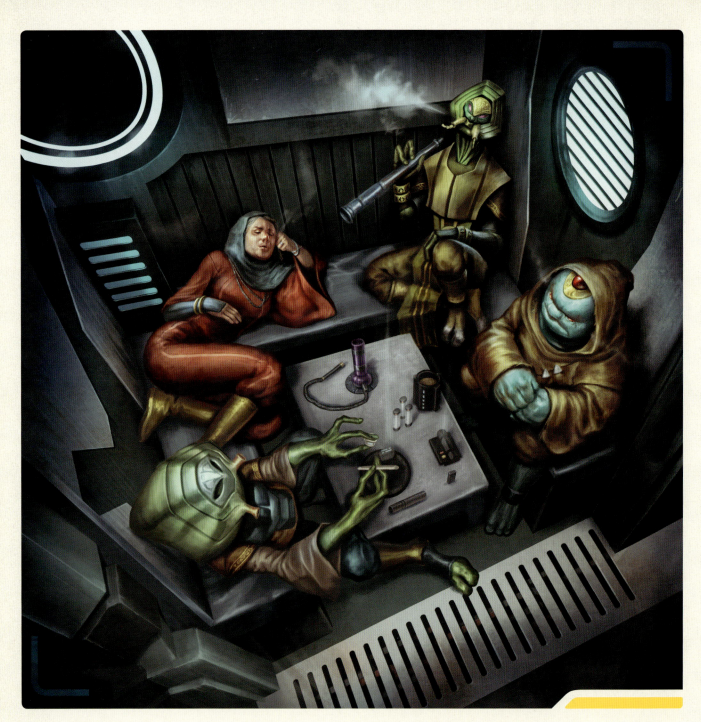

CORUSCANT LEVEL 3321 SPICE DEN SURVEILLANCE

A breakdown of cross-divisional cooperation along jurisdictional lines helped spread the scourge of spice addiction in Coruscant's undercity. The distant planet Kessel is a protectorate of the Pykes, untouched by the Republic. The Pykes, likewise, are an independent people based out of unincorporated Oba Diah. A long tradition of medical export treaties allowed for the transport of medicinal spice along legal channels, but the Pykes were profiting from less-documented spice transit. The illegal transporting resulted in a potent and deadly strain of refined spice spreading to the lower levels of the capital.

Pyke culture is forever tainted by this trade, with neighbors judging Pyke newcomers simply by what they've heard about the spice trade of their homeworld. Divo wrote:

I take no pleasure in casing a Pyke domicile, or barging into the back room of a Pyke restaurant or kitchen just because of who lives or works there. It is a rotten situation where these people have to bear the brunt of suspicion because someone far from them is getting rich from looking the other way.

Tach Drud ran a spice den out of a curio shop on Level 3321. The capture and interrogation of a spice-addled holo-star led law enforcement to Drud's shop in exchange for keeping the star's name out of the headlines. From Divo's notes:

Spice: the great equalizer. This undercover probe holo shows a senatorial lobbyist who pulls in a steep salary and a cargo hauler living just above squalor, united in their spiced-out stupor.

FILE / 7941.521.33

PORTRAIT OF LOM PYKE, SEIZED EVIDENCE

Found in the possession of Senator Yudrish Sedran of Chalacta, this portrait of Pyke capo Lom Pyke was said to be a cultural exchange gift from Oba Diah. However, Sedran was under investigation for claims that he was receiving bribes from the Pykes in exchange for turning a blind eye as they spread their operations beyond Pyke space as well as for granting limited diplomatic ambassadorial status, which gave Pyke delegates access to the Senate. Sedran's offices and apartments were sealed and their contents examined thoroughly for evidence of criminal activity. While his elite legal team was ultimately able to clear the senator of charges, this portrait proved to be a helpful piece of evidence. Tan Divo writes:

As clean as his books were, our esteemed senator couldn't wipe the grime of Pyke affiliation off everything in his office. Our forensic droids analyzed the Pyke paintings, and found grains of Kessel spice in the canvases velvet pile. Because spice has an organic core, each load of spice is unique and its markers serve as a fingerprint or a retina pattern that is traceable. The "signature" on the spice on Lom's portrait helped our sniffer droids and hound teams track down contraband at the 1313 docks.

YOUR NEIGHBORHOOD.
YOUR SAFETY.
YOUR TIRELESS POLICE SERVICE.
DEDICATED TO YOUR PROTECTION.

CONTACT LOCAL PRECINCT STATION FOR MORE INFORMATION ABOUT COMMUNITY RELATIONS AND FUNCTIONS

FILE / 7944.169.1

POLICE FORCE RECRUITMENT POSTER

During the Chancellery of Finis Valorum, a HoloNet News exposé revealed a streak of corruption in the highest levels of Republic politics due to senatorial ties to the Pyke Syndicate. Driven by spice profits, the criminal organization experienced explosive growth. Their newfound riches let them purchase favors from the capital, allowing them to muscle into territory that would otherwise be beyond their reach.

This move created a threat of all-out gang war in the depths of Coruscant. Despite Valorum's best efforts to hush this unrest while his administration tried to find a peaceful end to it, whisperings about a surge of lower-level violence wafted all the way to the surface.

Desperate to assure a skeptical public, Valorum tasked local politicians with spreading a message of law and order. The results were round-the-chrono holographic public service announcements and posters that cast a spotlight on the effective and efficient police departments on the city planet. The hope was that this would spur an increase in cadet enlistment. Though the results were negligible in the final analysis, these advertisements stayed in circulation for years, and are a cultural artifact of their time.

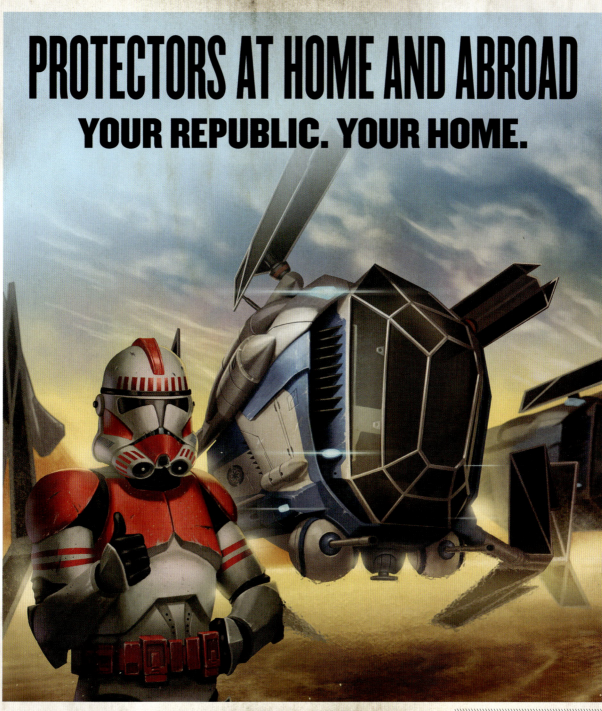

PROTECTORS AT HOME AND ABROAD
YOUR REPUBLIC. YOUR HOME.

CONTACT LOCAL PRECINCT STATIONS FOR OPPORTUNITIES TO CONTRIBUTE TO OUR SECURITY

FILE / 7957.910.3

SENATE DISTRICT LAW ENFORCEMENT RECRUITMENT POSTER

Shortly after the outbreak of the Clone Wars, imagery intended to recruit citizens into law enforcement changed in tenor and message from one of community service to one of military might. The rampant rise of a new military/industrial complex shaped nearly all government communications during the war. The clone trooper, though not specifically a law enforcement unit, became the face of Republic strength. This image, designed specifically to instill a sense of security and confidence in the Senate District following a calamitous bomb-ing, showcased the latest in military hardware.

Hovering behind the Phase II-armored clone trooper is a Santhe/Rothana LAAT/le gunship. Originally intended as a sleeker, low-cost alternative to the heavier battlefield LAAT/i model, this "police gunship" was pressed into civilian service on Coruscant and other Core World sector capitals. It had far more firepower than was normally assigned to law enforcement, but a skittish population living in fear of Separatist violence accepted the increase in armament hovering over their city streets in the name of security.

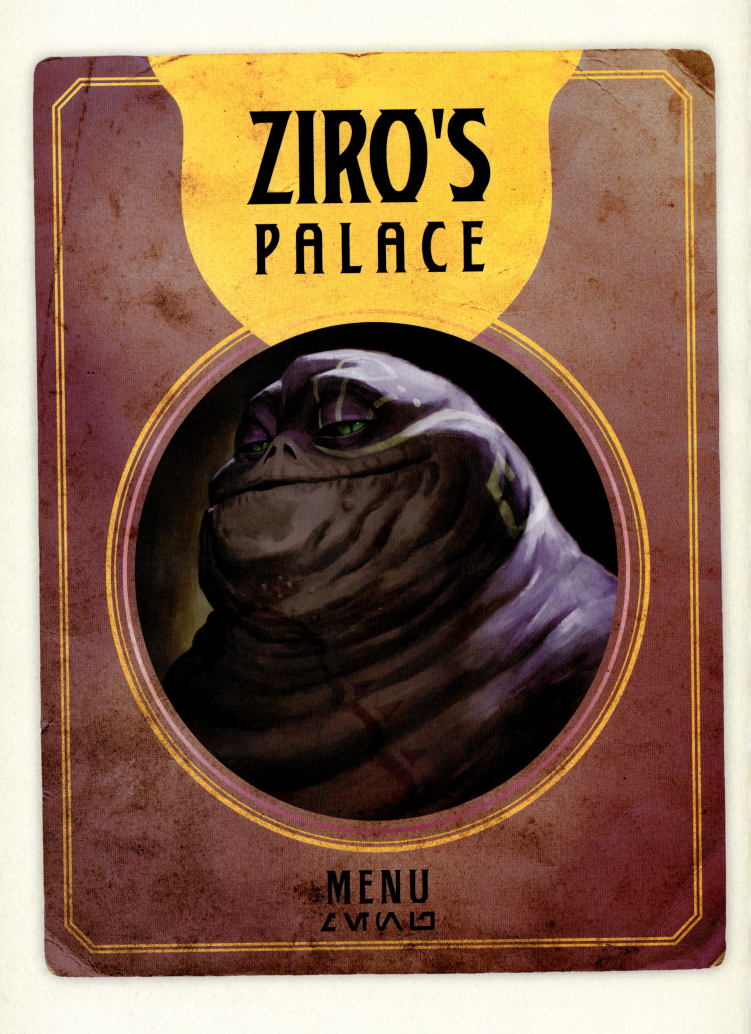

ZIRO'S
PALACE

MENU

FILE / 7947.923.1

ZIRO THE HUTT'S NIGHTCLUB MENU AND SURVEILLANCE

Ziro Desilijic Tiure was an outlier when it came to the Hutts' commerce ventures. Uncharacteristic of his species and culture, he established a business venue on Coruscant, far from Hutt Space. It was impolitic to accuse him of malfeasance while lacking evidence—such stereotyping was dangerous in so culturally mixed a world as the capital. Alas, it came as no surprise that Ziro the Hutt brought with him clientele that often skirted, and in some cases flouted, the law.

Before the Republic ever entered into a treaty with the Hutts, there were senators who had dealings with the Hutt kajidics—the clan-based businesses whose operations permeated the Outer Rim. Through front companies and other blinds, the Hutts lined the reelection coffers of politicians who treated their operations favorably. In a word, Ziro was *connected*. And the place to make these

connections was his nightclub, which clung to a wall of the Aradonti Ravine southwest of the Federal District.

On a handful of occasions, Divo's agents entered the nightclub, undercover, with concealed holocams. While this footage did not capture any illegal activity per se, it did make clear the powerful political clientele that frequented the club, and thus gave Divo some more leads to follow.

COMPILED SURVEILLANCE OF COCO TOWN EATERY DEX'S DINER

Located not far from the Federal District—and the Aradonti Ravine—was the Collective Commerce District, known colloquially as CoCo Town. It was far enough from Federal bustle, but close enough to be reachable by a short speeder jaunt during an extended lunch hour. Its location was also not far from Ziro's nightclub. Surveillance of the nightclub revealed a pattern: partners first acquainted at the posh nightclub would soon find themselves enjoying a no-frills meal at the twenty-four-hour eatery Dex's Diner. Divo wasn't one to credit coincidence, and began surveilling the diner. From his notes:

Dex is a good being. A checkered past, no doubt, but he's made amends and is making a clean living. It's no fault of his own that his open and welcoming nature attracts clientele of all stripes to his diner. Our investigations show no connection on his part to the deals cut at his tables. Though he wasn't overly cooperative with us because he didn't want his place tarred by a reputation for intruding into private affairs. I can respect that. We kept our distance, but we did keep an eye on the place.

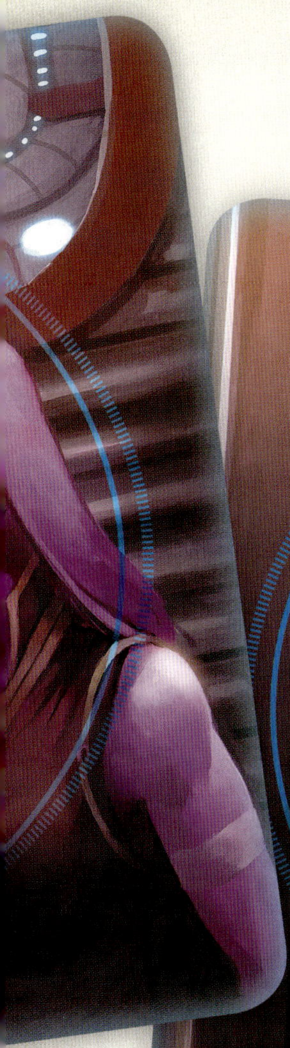

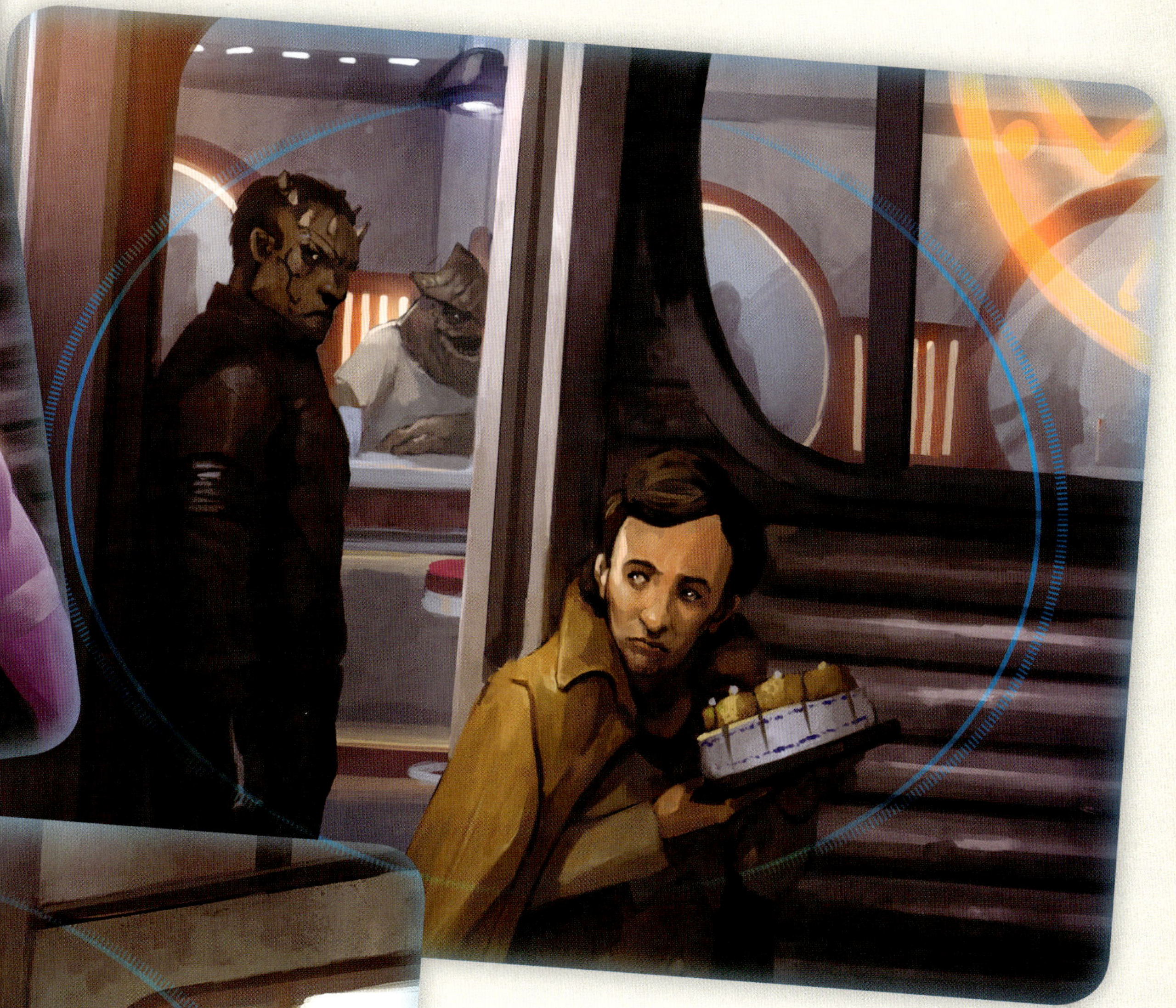

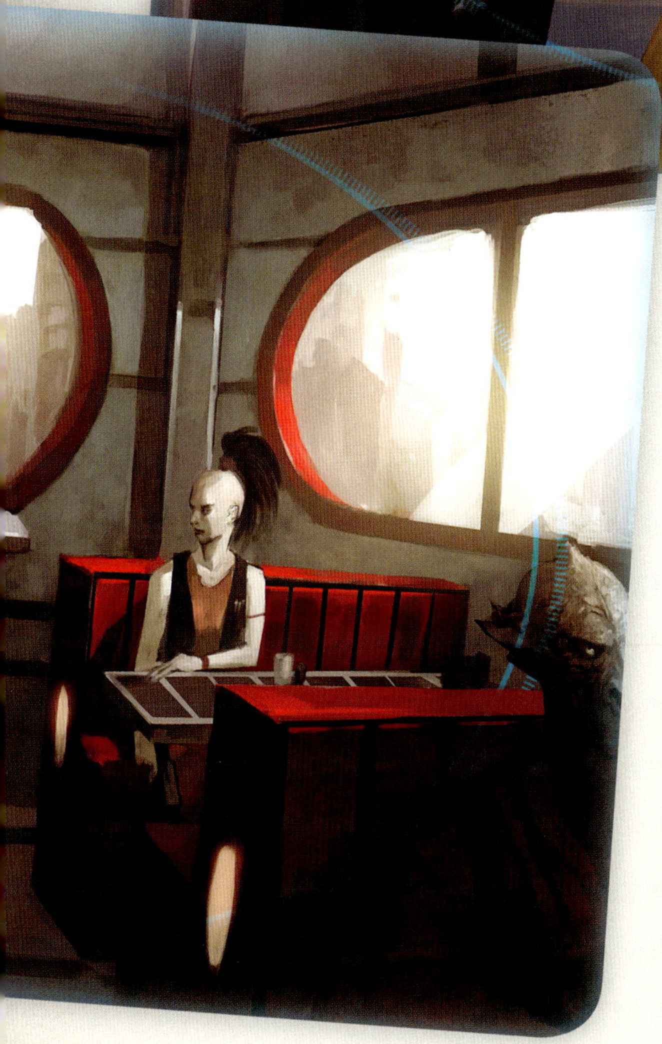

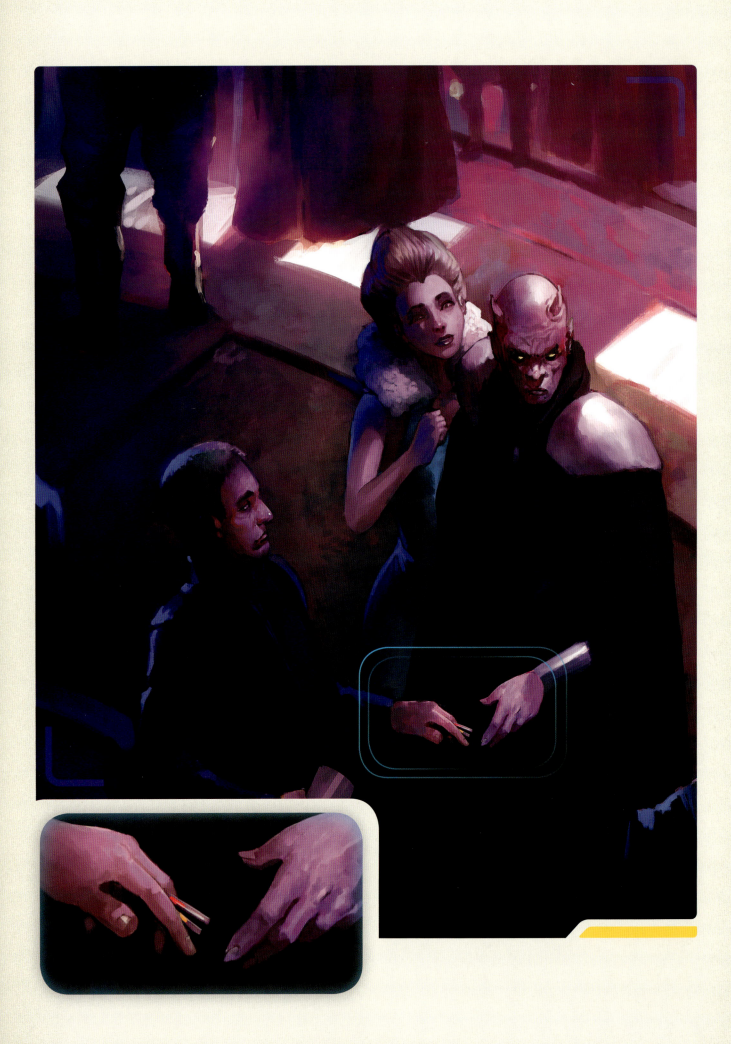

USCRU DISTRICT // LEVEL 3921 / ISSUING OFFICE / 3921.33.14

WARRANT

ᴏᴋ꒭꒭ᴋᴧ↓

STATUS:

PROCESSED

DANNL FAYTONNI

HEIGHT: 1.75M

GENDER: MALE

RACE: HUMAN

AGE: 54 STANDARD YEARS

FILE / 7955.811.4

DANNL FAYTONNI OUTLANDER SECURITY IMAGERY AND WARRANT

Divo kept a growing folder of incident reports involving a low-level con man named Dannl Faytonni, known to prowl the entertainment establishments of the Uscru District, particularly levels in the 4000s to mid-3000s range. Though Faytonni's greatest transgression was the impersonation of an officer of the Republic Judiciary, which triggered the issuing of a warrant for his arrest. Ultimately, it was not deemed a priority assignment as greater emphasis was placed on homeworld security in the wake of the Clone Wars. Nonetheless, Divo kept a remote eye on Faytonni, and encouraged the beat cops of the Uscru to do likewise. The ever-adaptive Faytonni found his niche while under such surveillance, offering up usable leads and fragmented information on larger quarry to the law in exchange for being able to continue his racket relatively unmolested.

With reservation, Divo allowed such leeway—as indicated by this holo of Faytonni selling spiced death sticks on the sly to a patron of the fashionable outlander nightclub. Divo notes:

I hate having to compromise in this way, but it's hard to argue that Faytonni is worth the fuel cells required to send a speeder down to fetch him, and he has a talent for washing his hands of crimes. But he'll mess up. They always do. And when he does, I'll be there.

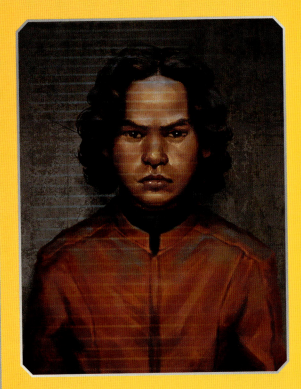
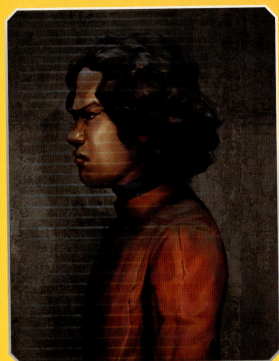

PRISON INTAKE FORM

FETT, BOBA

ᚢ᚛ᚔᚄᚑᚅ ᚔᚅᚂᚔᚊᚋᚑᚔ ᚏᚑᚌᚂ

FILE / 7956.103.1

BOBA FETT INTAKE HOLO

Among Tan Divo's files was a portfolio that tracked the early ascent of Boba Fett, long before Fett became the notorious bounty hunter of the Imperial era. Fett's criminal record began at the dawn of the Clone Wars, where he was identified as an accomplice in the attempted murder of Mace Windu, as well as in the bombing of the Star Destroyer *Endurance* over Vanqor. During processing, barristers argued that Fett was a subadult coerced by the true mastermind behind the plot—known criminal Aurra Sing. Some even argued that as a clone, he ceded his right to due process as he was property of the Galactic Republic, a by-product of the clone army agreement.

From Divo's notes:

This case keeps me up at night. This war is turning children into soldiers, but we can ignore that thanks to Kaminoans' age acceleration. But this is what an unaltered clone looks like, and can he really help who he is if he was molded to be this? I'm not alone in thinking this. A recommendation from General Windu suggested leniency and rehabilitation as opposed to corporal punishment, a request that ultimately fell on deaf ears in the Judiciary, who cited zero tolerance to attacks against military assets in this time of war.

FILE / 7956.103.2

EVIDENCE: BOMB SITE WRECKAGE/SALVAGED MANDALORIAN HELMET

Pulled from the smoldering wreckage of the *Endurance* Star Destroyer, dashed on the crystalline surface of Vanqor, was this perfectly bisected fragment of authentic Mandalorian armor. Metallurgical analysis confirmed its composition to be beskar with unparalleled purity. Testimony from Jedi Master Mace Windu confirmed its previous owner as the late Jango Fett.

At the start of the Clone Wars, Windu was forced to kill Fett in self-defense, an act committed before the impressionable eyes of Fett's young son, Boba. Though Boba's whereabouts were unknown following the chaotic outbreak of the war, he had infiltrated the ranks of junior clone cadets, and came within striking distance of Windu on multiple occasions aboard the *Endurance*.

After having downed the destroyer—an act of sabotage that rivaled some of the most egregious in the war—Fett next left his father's helmet as a lure to Windu. Encased within the helmet was a shaped baradium charge. Though Windu and General Anakin Skywalker survived the explosion, they were trapped beneath rubble for hours. As evidence of beskar's remarkable kinetic dissipation properties, the helmet fragments remain remarkably intact.

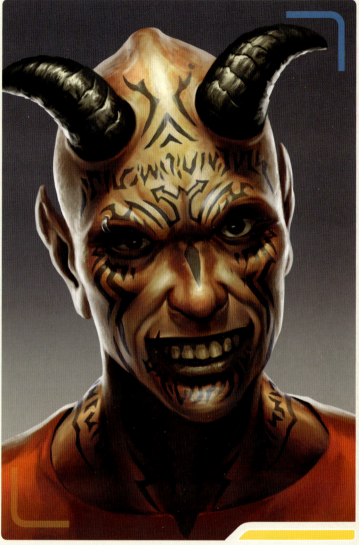

FILE / 7959.222.4

CRIMINAL INTAKE PHOTOS; DERMAL COMPARISONS

Intended as a sign of deep commitment, certain criminal gangs brand their heritage and affiliation as dermal embellishments—specific scarification and/or tattoos. The more elaborate the markings, in most cases, the more deeply entrenched and storied the criminal's history. Profiling tattoo markings for potential criminality is troublesome, as it can be a legitimate cultural artifact for some species, and wearing such markings themselves is not criminal. It is a circumstantial filter that may heighten security if certain imagery trips automatic pattern-recognizing sensors, or is spotted by seasoned officers in the field.

In a few instances, tattoos have a practical criminal application. There are reports in Divo's files of electro-conductive pigment patterns that can hold data, making the skin pattern a vehicle for the smuggling of confiscated information.

The Imperial Office of Criminal Investigation inherited vast troves of records regarding tattoo symbology. Divo suggested a program of deploying protocol droids that specialize in tattoo recognition for use in crowded spaceports and transit areas. The Imperial Security Bureau implemented his recommendations within the first years of the Empire.

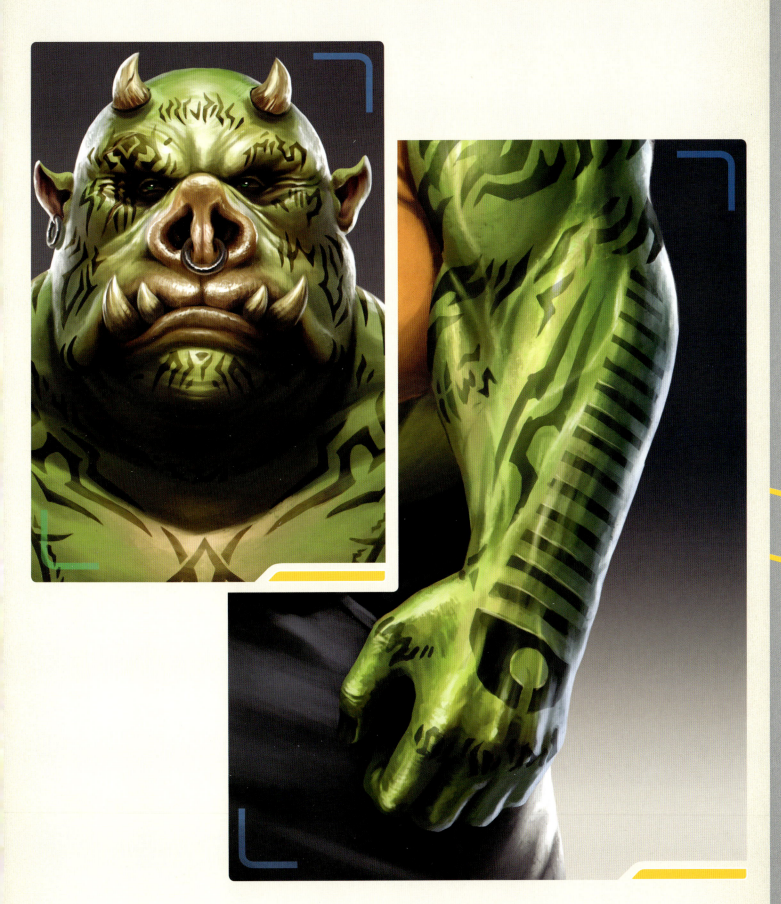

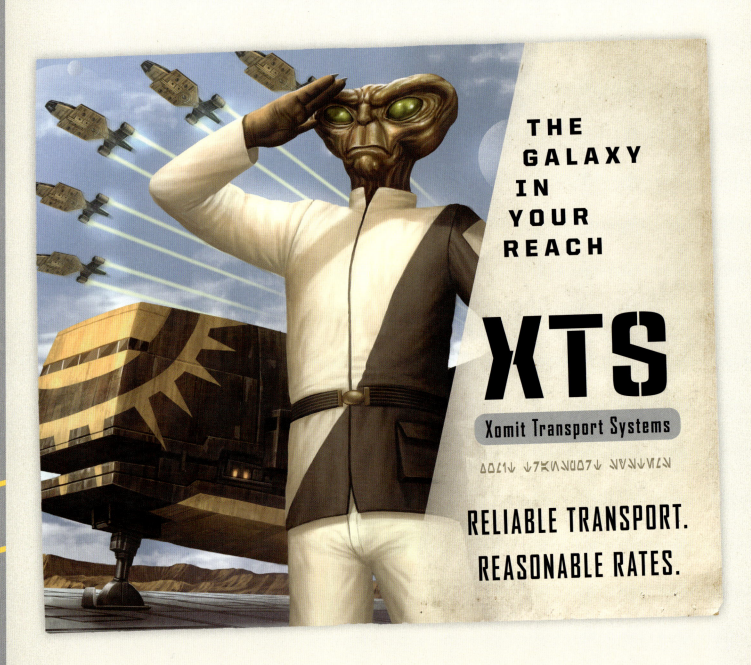

THE
GALAXY
IN
YOUR
REACH

XTS

Xomit Transport Systems

RELIABLE TRANSPORT.
REASONABLE RATES.

FILE / 7953.231.1

FILEADVERT FOR XOMIT TRANSPORT SYSTEMS

It's usually street crime that is the focus of dramatized and romanticized depictions of law enforcement, but its impact on society and scale of crime pales in comparison to corporate crime. Shielded by impenetrable layers of datawork, graft, and legal defense, big business operates with frustrating impunity. It becomes an "open secret" in precincts that corporations are crooked, with cops lamenting that they are only able to catch the street punks, while the big nested kings and queens remain untouched in their skyrise palaces.

Xomit Transport Systems, based out of Falleen with a major regional hub on Mustafar, was connected to many incidents of contraband smuggling. Believed to be masterminded by the Black Sun syndicate, XTS (for Xomit Transport Systems) had the protection of wealthy trading guilds with senators in their pockets. Several times a path of clues that could have blown a case wide open would lead to the locked cargo doors of an XTS freighter, turning the clues cold with implacable permits and waivers.

From Divo's notes during the Clone Wars:

A measure was proposed this week by Chancellor Palpatine to heavily restrict the coaxium markets, thus parceling out hyperspace fuels to transport agencies that met specific law enforcement standards and agreements, but the merchant guilds opposed it. Here is a situation where we have to wait for the politicians to fight it out and in the meantime we have our hands tied.

With the death of chairman Xomit Grunseit during the Clone Wars, it is unclear who on the reformed XTS board became its new leader.

FILE / 7951.313.6

QUINLAN VOS SURVEILLANCE IMAGE

Though Divo had his documented differences with the Jedi Council, there was one Jedi whom he took care to laud in his reports: Quinlan Vos. Vos was the Jedi Order's interface with local law enforcement, and the point man in the Jedi's exploration of criminal activity within the Core Worlds and beyond. Vos demonstrated respect for police, commiserating with them on the Republic's shortcomings, openly sharing intel with even the smallest precincts, and sometimes having an ale with them at the corner "cop cantina" in the sketchiest neighborhoods. While other Jedi seemed unapproachable and inscrutable, Vos was quite the opposite.

The Clone Wars removed Vos from his regular beat, as the needs of the war had him focus on larger movements of materiel connected to the Republic's efforts to defeat the Separatists. Vos handed over much of the groundwork and data he had compiled on the roots of organized crime in the lower levels of Coruscant to the local department heads.

Vos is presumed dead, implicated in the Jedi insurrection to overthrow the Republic. Divo remained silent on such matters.

PRISONER

HARDEEN, RAKO

ꓶꓶꓶꓶꓶꓶ ꓶꓶꓶꓶꓶꓶꓶ ꓶꓶꓶꓶꓶ

FILE / 7956.901.3

"RAKO HARDEEN" INTAKE HOLO

The case of Rako Hardeen exemplifies the strain often felt between local law enforcement and the galactic judicial work carried out by the Jedi Order. The Jedi have traditionally been given a large remit in their operations, with open access to police intelligence and groundwork. For centuries, it was a two-way path. Then the Clone Wars struck, and such access evaporated.

From Divo's notes:

I had been assembling a case against Hardeen for years. The so-called Marksman of Concord Dawn was a bounty hunter reputed to be taking extralegal cases. His visits to Coruscant meant my case file was updated often, but I could

never crack it. Then, one morning I got an unexpected alert: he had been arrested by the Jedi. He was being held at the Jedi Temple, but I was denied access to him.

Even upon Hardeen's transfer to the Republic Judiciary Central Detention Center, my requests to interview him or examine the Jedi arrest reports were denied. I eventually received a heavily redacted report of Hardeen accepting a bounty on a Jedi Council member, and his assassination of Obi-Wan Kenobi on behalf of a redacted employer. This should have been an opportunity to bring down whoever was propping Hardeen up, but the Jedi refused to share their intelligence.

Within the week, I learned that Kenobi was alive, having posed as Hardeen to infiltrate the prison community. This intake holograph of Hardeen is not of Hardeen at all. Kenobi's prison stint was cut short by a prison break that allowed dozens of hardened criminals to escape into the Coruscant streets. And all of this was part of a sting operation meant to reveal a plot against the Supreme Chancellor's life—and yet the Supreme Chancellor's office had no record of it!

Whose side are they on?

Whatever became of the real Rako Hardeen is a secret the Jedi Order took to the grave.

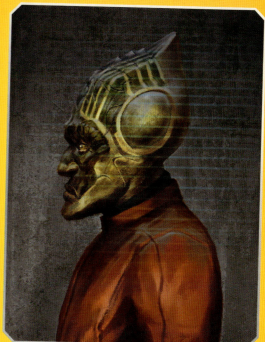

PRISONER

EVAL, MORALO

꒰ꁝ꒱ Aurebesh text ꒱

FILE / 7956.881.4

MORALO EVAL INTAKE HOLO

One of the most loathsome criminals in the Republic, Moralo Eval had sociopathic tendencies and violent criminal behavior. Despite the Phindian reverence for family, Eval murdered his mother in cold blood, claiming that he was "bored." The Phindians had no way of dealing with such a transgression. Their compassionate attempts to understand the underpinnings of such behavior—rather than punish him for his crimes—led to lax security conditions that allowed him to escape. Eval was a serial murderer who avoided the law with a crafty brilliance. Over the years, he established a reputation as a deranged genius.

After being captured by a police detachment on Denon, Eval was remanded into Coruscant custody, where he was sentenced to maximum security at Republic Judiciary Central Detention Center. An (at the time) inexplicable processing error placed him in contact with other prisoners, rather than keeping him confined to solitary. This is what led to a breakout, which turned out to be facilitated, to some degree, by the Jedi.

The Jedi risked an awful lot, and I doubt I'll ever get a full picture of what this operation entailed. The Chancellor told me that this whole elaborate operation was a Jedi bid to stop an assassination attempt on his life, engineered by Eval from behind prison walls. The Chancellor was sympathetic to my incredulity, and told me of his concerns that the Jedi did not include me in planning this. The Chancellor definitely seemed tired by these events, and struck me as so vulnerable when he imparted his growing unease with Jedi independence in matters of the war.

WANTED

NAME:

Cad Bane

HEIGHT: 1.85M

GENDER: MALE

SPECIES: DUROS

AGE: 41 STANDARD YEARS (ESTIMATE)

ISSUING PLANET

CORUSCANT

THE REPUBLIC IS SEEKING THE CAPTURE OF THIS FUGITIVE

FILE / 7956.901.3

CAD BANE WANTED POSTER

Law enforcement has always endured a tumultuous relationship with bounty hunters. Under ideal circumstances, bounty hunters are licensed and authorized law enforcers, pursuing wanted criminals in exchange for a legally posted reward. But in practice, the hunters' license has often become a permit to break the law. Frequently, a bounty hunter is a gun-for-hire first, and law enforcer second, if that. Hunters follow the money. They have little compunction about operating clearly on the wrong side of the law.

Cad Bane had been the subject of close examination by Divo, since the Duros bounty hunter rocketed in notoriety and prominence following the disappearance of Jango Fett. In circles that debate such things, Bane had ascended to the rank of "best bounty hunter in the business." Bane's bounty-hunting certification allowed him to carry heavy weap-onry on occasion, and collateral damage was common in his hunts. It was not until he moved directly against Jedi interests that he was collared by the Judicials, and thrown into the Republic Judiciary Central Detention Center. Divo's single note appended to Bane's intake holo:

He seems pretty confident he is getting out of there.

FILE / 7956.221.4

KRAYT'S CLAW POSSE SURVEILLANCE IMAGE

Divo's fascination with Boba Fett continued after the young man's escape from the Republic Judiciary Central Detention Center (see FILE 7956.901.3). A fugitive from Republic law, Fett avoided activity in Republic space, and stayed mostly in unincorporated territories in the Outer Rim for xthe remainder of the war (though occasional rumors of him on Coruscant did certainly pique Divo's interest).

A police constable from Mos Eisley contacted Divo in the last year of the war with a holographic image touting the services of the Krayt's Claw, a posse of bounty hunters based out of Tatooine. Divo wrote:

It's the kid. The jogan doesn't roll far from the vine, as they say. He's taken up the bounty hunter trade, no doubt following in his father's footsteps. And rather than lying low, he's leaning on his father's reputation by broadcasting his name: Fett. He's got big shoes to fill, and I don't like the looks of who he's partnering with. Will have to do more research.

The other hunters would subsequently be identified as Embo, Bossk, C-21 Highsinger, Dengar, Aurra Sing, and Latts Razzi, all of whom would receive dedicated files within Divo's dossiers.

RECONSTRUCTED IMAGE OF THE XREXUS CARTEL TRAFFICKING

The Xrexus Cartel was a collection of semi-legitimate droid manufacturing firms from the Mid Rim that banded together to fix prices and distribute unlicensed combat automata imported from the Outer Rim. They came to Divo's attention when a shipment of sham Xrexus restraining bolts surfaced on Coruscant as part of a planned droid uprising ordered by the Glitch, a splinter of the infamous Droid Gotra syndicate.

Divo's files called the Xrexus case "a maddening dead end," because their activities—and their founder Xev Xrexus—"vanished as if gobbled by a black hole" about a decade before the First Galactic Empire Day. It remained a cold case until the detainment of KRONOS-841, a Gotra droid captured by Imperial forces in their first year.

Divo oversaw the interrogation of KRONOS-841, and in exchange for leniency, the droid offered up a data dump of pertinent memories—over a decade old—of what appeared to be Xrexus auctioning a captured Jedi Padawan named Eldra Kaitis. Though KRONOS and his cohorts were bidding by proxy, they were outbid by the industrialist Jee Kra, who offered 2.5 million credits for Kaitis. It is here where KRONOS's evidence ends.

Research by Divo uncovered that Kra was found dead in a shuttle crash beyond the Republic borders, and that any further investigation into his death would be closed by the office of the Supreme Chancellor during the Clone Wars for classified reasons. Divo writes:

Near as I can tell, the Jedi had no record of whatever became of Eldra Kaitis. By the time I got KRONOS's data, there were no Jedi left to report this discovery to. I can only assume she died, and that perhaps Xrexus's disappearance was due to "Jedi business" that was never reported to any other agencies.

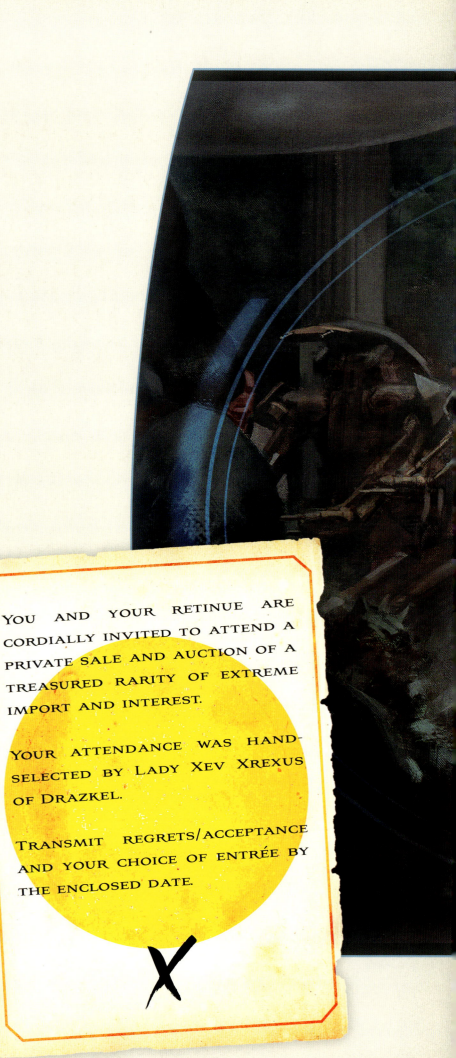

YOU AND YOUR RETINUE ARE CORDIALLY INVITED TO ATTEND A PRIVATE SALE AND AUCTION OF A TREASURED RARITY OF EXTREME IMPORT AND INTEREST.

YOUR ATTENDANCE WAS HAND-SELECTED BY LADY XEV XREXUS OF DRAZKEL.

TRANSMIT REGRETS/ACCEPTANCE AND YOUR CHOICE OF ENTRÉE BY THE ENCLOSED DATE.

FILE / 7956.319.3

CONJECTURAL HIERARCHY OF THE SHADOW COLLECTIVE

During the Clone Wars, a rash of violence and suspicious reallocation of funds and capital led to the discovery of a short-lived but expansive criminal syndicate known only as the Shadow Collective. The Collective was believed to have funded the toppling of Duchess Satine's government on Mandalore, which threw the planet into chaos.

UNKNOWN

HUTT CARTEL
(Tatooine)
Jabba Dislijic Tiure

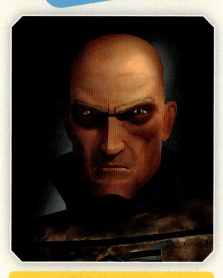

DEATH WATCH
(Nomadic)
Pre Vizsla

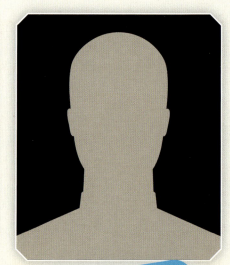

UNKNOWN

PYKE SYNDICATE
(Oba Diah)
Lom Pyke

BLACK SUN
(Mustafar)
Ziton Moj

FILE / 7956.221.4

UNDERCOVER HOLOGRAPH: THE MEETING OF THE HUTTS

Among the records uncovered in Divo's files was material that would, ultimately, have been inadmissible had any legal action been taken against suspects. The laws of the Republic did not extend to the sovereign territory of Hutt Space, but the business interests of the Hutts did probe deeply into the Republic's regions. This double standard tied the law's hands, as Hutts and their agents could conveniently disappear across borders.

The Clone Wars could have changed this, as a treaty was forged with the Hutts to allow Republic access to otherwise private Outer Rim trade routes. But again the hands of law enforcement officials were tied by legal and political matters. Divo wrote:

Republic legal scholars grossly underestimated the jurisprudence of the Hutts. Their lawyers amended the treaty to such a degree that they could peek into

our side of the fence, and we could not do the same.

Law enforcement did what it could within the narrow margins the agencies were given. This image was captured from a translator droid, gifted via a third party to the Hutt Grand Council on Nal Hutta. While none of the imagery here could be used against the Hutts in a legal sense, it at least allowed a heads-up as to some of their nefarious plans.

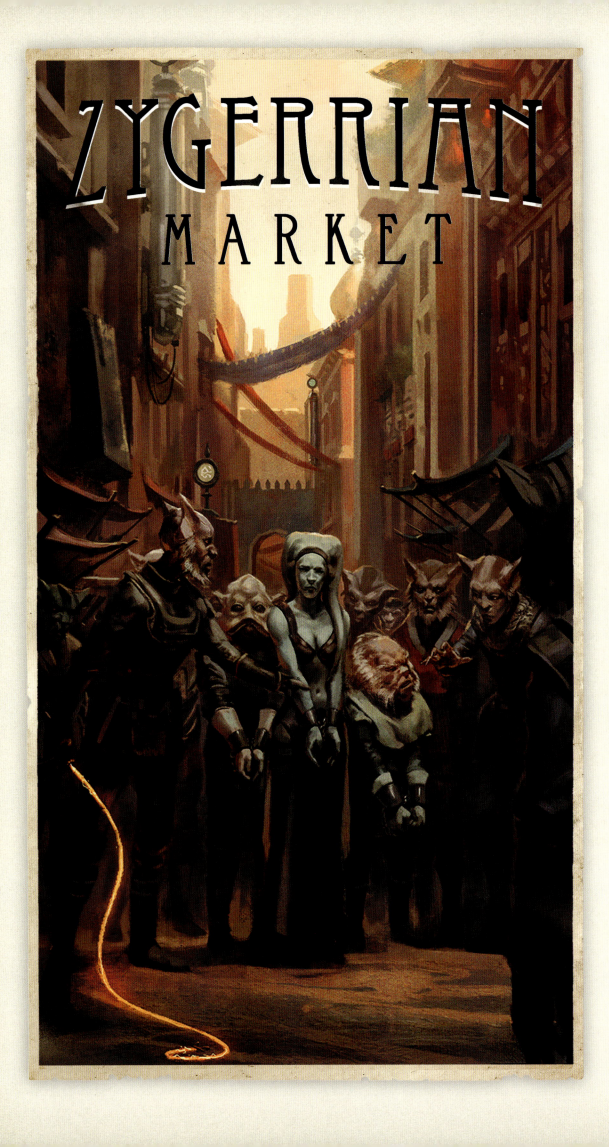

◄ FILE / 7956.919.5

ZYGERRIAN SLAVE MARKET FLYER

Despite uniting thousands of worlds and stretching for tens of thousands of light-years, the Republic was often criticized for being insular by those within and without its borders. Neighboring independent states flouted Republic laws that could not reach them, acting as a beacon for the unscrupulous and as a haven for fugitives.

Slavery, the most despicable of trades, prospered in the lawlessness of the Outer Rim. The Hutts dabbled in this business, even after their alignment with the Republic during the Clone Wars. Whatever else may be said for the Hutts, their interest in slavery was minor compared to that of the Zygerrians. The Zygerrians were driven by more than profit—they felt a cultural entitlement to slave trade, for it was the Zygerrians who built a vast empire in pre-Republic times on the backs of sentient beings they treated like chattel.

When word of youths being captured and trafficked out of Coruscant to the Outer Rim reached Divo, his network of contacts were able to point to Zygerria as the ultimate destination. The Zygerrians, emboldened by the fractured Republic of the Clone Wars, returned their underground slave trade to the surface, preying upon unfortunate souls displaced by the war. Zygerria's independence limited the actions the Republic could take against it, and it was not until the slavers tipped their hands to being accomplices to the Separatist Alliance that a liberation effort was launched as part of a military strike.

FILE / 7956.919.5 ▲

ZYGERRIAN SLAVER'S WHIP

Found in a captured shipping container holding twenty-seven subadults from Coruscant, Corellia, and Denon, this Zygerrian slaver's whip was kept as evidence in Divo's possession. The articulated electro-whip has a retractable coiled conductive filament that carries a voltaic plasma charge capable of dispensing painful electric shocks that could induce paralyzing neurological seizures. Though electrified whips are not unique to the Zygerrians, the Zygerrian whip design is distinctive and considered the most painful and potentially deadly of such subjugation tools.

FILE / 7944.111.3

ANNOTATED PUBLICITY HOLO OF SEBULBA OF PIXELITO

An attempt by Zugga Entertainment to open a podrace course in the Grand Aratech Gravidrome on Coruscant led Divo to amass volumes of research on the sport because the spectacle's shady reputation raised his suspicions. While long associated with the Outer Rim, podracing was, at the time, growing in popularity in the Core Worlds. The podrace course never happened, possibly because Zugga got wind that law enforcement was taking an interest.

Lieutenant Divo's internal correspondence to his section chief included this appended holograph of racing champion Sebulba of Pixelito:

This is what passes as a "hero" in these circuits. Even from the most cursory of research, it's clear he's crooked. Funding pours into these races from sponsors such as Czerka, Mekuun, and Collar Pondrat, corporations long suspected of laundering funds in the Outer Rim. Beyond the imagery captured in holo-broadcasts, it is easy to see how lawless and deadly this sport is. Some people claim the sport is fake and the drama is engineered for the cameras. But the risk is real and lethal. I could, with minimal effort, point to leads that identify Sebulba as hiring racecourse assassins. But he's a hero. There are kids with toys and posters of the Dug. It's a relief to know trash like this won't set foot in our town, and kids here won't be holding up this miscreant as some sort of idol.

FILE / 7945.313.2

HIDDEN HOLOGRAPHY: PODRACE CHICANERY

Submitted to Divo anonymously, as a tardy addendum to his research into podracing-related crimes, was a hologram that alleges to answer the mystery of whatever became of Neva Kee, rising star of the Baroonda Circuit. Kee vanished during the Boonta Eve Podrace of '945 (C.R.C. date), disappearing entirely during a stretch of the race conspicuously not covered by holographic cam

droids. Rumors propagated by *Podracing Quarterly* suggested he fled the race with his experimental podracer in an impulsive rush to avoid creditors.

The signature authentimarks on the hologram have been scrubbed, making it impossible to confirm the image. But if true, it depicts Jabba the Hutt paying off Aurra Sing while his cronies drag an incapacitated Kee from the site of

a crash. The Mos Espa case officer investigating the matter had hit a dead end, and reached out to Divo for help. Divo's theory, updated years after the incident, was that Farwan & Glott, the original manufacturers of Kee's podracer, arranged the hit to get their hands on Kee's customization secrets—modifications he otherwise refused to share.

Fellow traveler,

It is I, Hondo Ohnaka, of the esteemed Ohnaka Gang of Pirates, Privateers, and Freebooters, who has claimed and commandeered your vessel for the advancement of my legacy. Please rest assured that no harm will come to you, for you are a vital part in the spread of my legend. My crew, such as they are, will review your cargo and belongings, and abscond with what we deem worthy additions to our larder. Your weapons and propulsion systems will be temporarily disabled in such a manner that you, being of reasonable skill, will be able to restore within hours of our departure. Your life-support systems will remain unaffected, provided you in no way threaten our operations. Let us all be civilized.

While a simple electronic transmission would have sufficed, I have included durasheet copies of this letter so as to provide a more permanent record of our interaction for your files. It is sure to become a collector's item, my friend. I realize I may be putting you out financially by apprehending your cargo, but consider this gift a means of getting new footing in life, a life that has been touched by Hondo Ohnaka.

Clear skies!

FILE / 7957.338.1

HONDO OHNAKA "LETTERS" AND SURVEILLANCE IMAGE

After a rash of piracy along the Metellos Trade Route, the route leading to Coruscant, landed on Divo's scanners, he put out an interdivisional call for any information regarding Weequay raiders, based on what scant evidence there was. A torrent of reports flooded his receptacle, with one name constantly popping up: Hondo Ohnaka.

Ohnaka avoided the inner worlds, most likely the result of enemies he had made in his long and checkered life, but he certainly covered vast areas in the Mid and Outer Rims. The Ohnaka gang was based out of Florrum, largely specializing in low-risk salvage punctuated by the occasional hostile capture of ships and passengers for ransom. An analysis of the Ohnaka files—including the enclosed "letters of marque" attributed to the pirate—showed a lack of political convictions among the Ohnaka gang. During the Clone Wars, they were a nuisance to the Republic and the Separatists alike, going so far as to kidnap the leader of the Separatist state.

Though Divo's call for information resulted in a flood of requests, warrants, and rewards for the capture of Ohnaka from outlying agencies, the inspector ultimately never responded. Ohnaka kept to the frontier for the remainder of the Republic's days, and seemed to know better than to tangle with Imperial might in the decades that followed.

KRAYT'S CLAW UPDATE

Another holo was forwarded to Tan Divo, attached to an annual Life Day greeting from Constable Sedra Hoxin from the Mos Eisley prefect's office. The note attached said, "Sir. A gift. An update. Someone's growing up."

Divo wrote:

He's not just partnering. He's leading. I didn't realize it before, but Fett's in charge of the Krayt's Claw. He's handling the business. Old enough to cut deals, but probably not old enough to drink in that cantina. He has holes to fill—a childhood lost and a father killed—and is turning to a life as a bounty hunter. I suppose it could be worse.

This is the last record Divo has of Boba Fett in his archives.

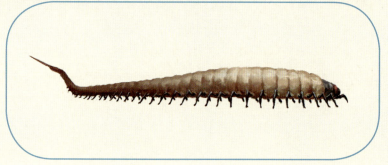

FILE / 7955.442.1

EVIDENCE: ASSASSINATION ATTEMPT ON SENATOR AMIDALA

On the eve of the controversial Galactic Senate vote on the Military Creation Act, Senator Padmé Amidala of the Chommel sector was the target of no less than two assassination attempts. The first was an early dawn bombing on her delegation landing platform, which killed seven in Amidala's retinue. This led to a postponement of the vote. Later that same night, the would-be killer struck again, using distinct tools of the trade that—after some negotiation with the investigating Jedi Knights—Divo was able to secure for further study.

The assassin, later identified as Zam Wesell, used an ASN droid (see evidence image on right) to insert a pair of venomous arthropods into Amidala's sleeping quarters—a location left vulnerable by the senator's insistence that her surveillance equipment be shut down in the name of privacy. The image of the incident is a spectrum-shifted reconstruction derived from passive EM records gathered from a low-powered astromech droid that was in the room at the time.

The bisected remains of the creatures, each split in two by a laser sword, were identified as *Indoumodo kouhuns* by myriapodologists from the Coruscant Zoo. They have been preserved as evidence (see canister to the left) and have had their venom sacks removed in hopes of being able to concoct an antivenin.

Though Divo's notes credit Amidala's head of security, Captain Gregar Typho, for his fast-acting response in calling local law enforcement, his records have little to say about Jedi cooperation on the matter. This added note underlines Divo's chronic frustration about interagency coordination.

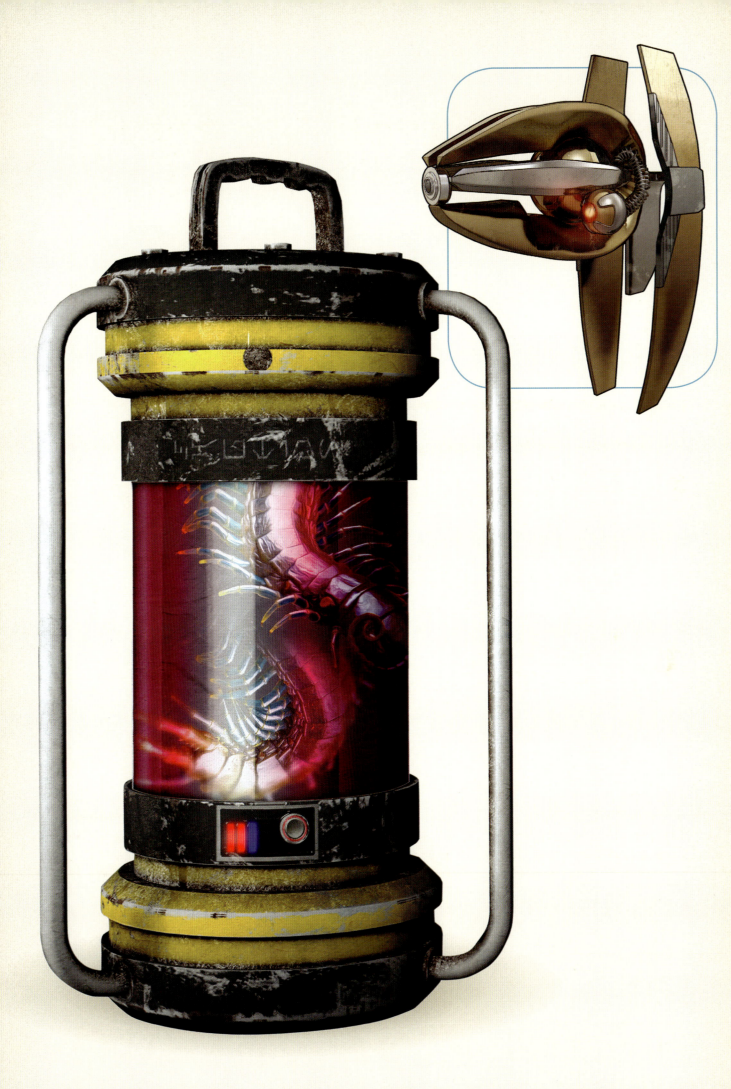

46

CRIME SCENE EVIDENCE, NACK MOVERS'S RESIDENCE

A hit man, "cleaner," and eliminator of loose ends in the criminal underworld, Nack Movers had a talent for covering his tracks. Attempts to pin a string of dead informants, accountants, and even a crooked cop on him were stymied by payoffs or witness and prosecutor intimidation. Someone was looking out for Movers, ensuring he had a comfortable life in a skyrise apartment on the upper east side of the Jrade District.

In his notes, Divo commented:

I would have wanted justice to catch up to him, and in a sense it did. But not from us. From someone he took for granted.

Movers's paranoia led him to hire a Terellian jango jumper named Cassilyda "Cassie" Cryar as a bodyguard and assistant. The lecherous Trandoshan propositioned Cryar in a manner far from professional, despite entreaties from his live-in girlfriend, Ione Marcy. What Movers failed to notice is how close Cryar and Marcy had grown, and that the two were plotting against him.

Movers's professional weapon was poison, having apparently been trained as a Malkite poisoner. Traces of Sennari were found in his bloodstream, administered via drink. The reaction of his Trandoshan physiology to the toxin led him to convulse violently, knocking over furniture before finally collapsing in a heap. An examination of claw marks across a painting of happier times matches Movers's talons.

Again, from Divo's notes:

Live this way, Nack, die this way.

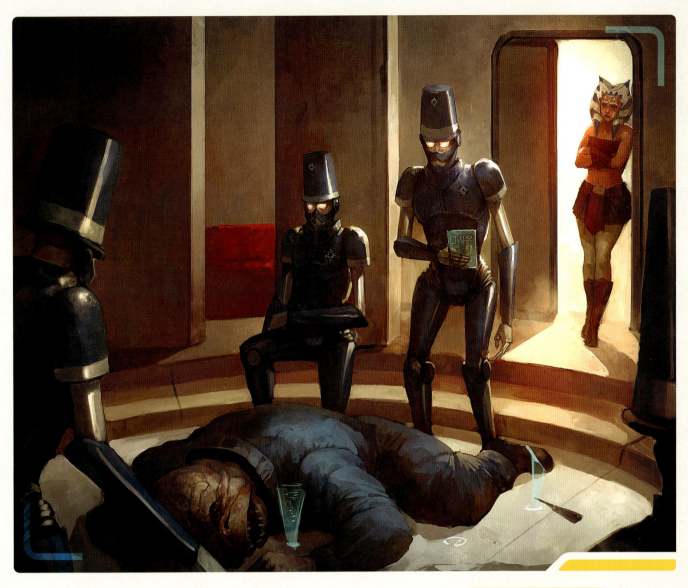

▲ FILE / 7956.101.2

CRIME SCENE EVIDENCE, NACK MOVERS'S RESIDENCE

Analysis droid Russo-ISC (evidence logged here) crime scene examination report, blood sample analysis.

» SUBJECT: Movers, Nack
» ID: COR143817TRND195441.37
» HEIGHT: 1.75 meters
» WEIGHT: 104 kg
» ANALYSIS: 155 Na; 5.2 K; 6.4 Urea; 130 Creatinine; 130 Glucose; 33 Cu
» CONTAMINANTS: Sennari extract 11.3

JEDI HANGAR BOMBING FORENSIC ANALYSIS

A shocking terrorist strike at the heart of the Jedi Temple crystallized just how unpopular the Clone Wars had become on Coruscant, sparking protests around the Jedi Temple to demand an end to the war.

Within the temple launch facilities, a nanodroid-triggered carbon bomb killed twelve crew workers, eight clones, six Jedi, and wounded dozens more. This sensor composite of the crime scene was assembled by combining data from security sensors as well as efficiency and safety monitors that covered the hangar facility. These streams of data were holographically projected over the bombing site so a detailed, in-context analysis of the explosive event could be conducted. Investigators could walk through varying vantage points of the bomb site, and throttle backward and forward in the timeline of the event to piece together the chain of events. In this way, crime scene analyzer Russo-ISC along with Jedi General Anakin Skywalker and Commander Ahsoka Tano were able to confirm the bomb originated inside the body of compromised crew member Jackar Bowmani, a munitions expert cleared for access.

48

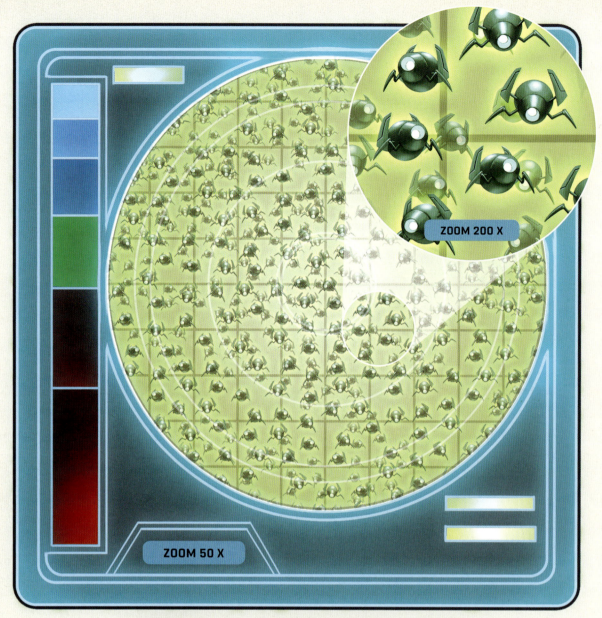

ZOOM 200 X

ZOOM 50 X

FILE / 7957.211.0

NANODROID EVIDENCE, POST-TRIAL SUBMISSION

Insidious weapons so small they escape notice except from dedicated sensors, nanodroids were prohibited by Republic law outside controlled and monitored industrial applications. Their destructive potential has been known for decades. These droids, technically NM-K reconstitutors, are 1.5 nanometers in length, and are primarily used in the fabrication of advanced electronics. They are kept in a suspension of electrolytic transfer fluid, and are typically applied to a raw material work area with a swab or roller.

The reconstitutors, however, when subverted by illegal programming, take on a new role. At a molecular level, they can reconstitute carbon-based matter to explosively unstable configurations. In this way, they can turn unwitting beings into walking time bombs. This gruesome tactic was used by former Jedi terrorist Barriss Offee in the bombing of the Jedi Temple late into the Clone Wars.

What was to be a strictly internal Jedi investigation fell beyond their domain into military court due to the death of clone troopers in the explosion. The police were largely kept out of the investigation, though intelligence was shared with Inspector Divo after a verdict had already been delivered against the bomber. In addition to a heavily redacted report, Divo was given access to a nullified sample of NM-Ks, and a compressed baryon canister used to smuggle them.

FILE / 7956.123.2

CONFISCATED MOOGAN TEA

Several pallets of Moogan tea from the Ardees Beverage Company were confiscated at the Eastport Docks on Coruscant thanks to a tip from the Sundari Police Authority on Mandalore, an atypical heads-up from a world known for its independence. Divo notes:

Cops can talk to cops, and in this case, we put politics aside in the matter of public safety.

Mandalore had suffered an outbreak of poisoning due to black marke-teers taking advantage of the supply shortage created by the Clone Wars. Making the crime particularly egregious was that the tainted beverage was specifically sold to schools for distribution to children. The Moogan smuggler Tee Va had acquired concentrate from an inside source within the beverage company, and found a way to extend its shelf life by mixing the concentrate with inexpensive slabin, a potentially dangerous additive if not used correctly.

Mandalorian Police Captain Patrok Ru-Saxon helped Duchess Satine Kryze expose the plot. A review of the Moogan transport ship's navi-computer records indicated a stop off on Coruscant, suggesting that they were looking to open a market there. Ru-Saxon's tip led Divo to a shipment destined for the Coruscant underlevels that was intercepted before it could do any harm.

As a show of thanks, Divo sent Ru-Saxon a bottle of artisanal Tarine tea from Coruscant, and received a bottle of Mandalorian kri'gee ale in turn.

THE TIME OF THE EMPIRE

The galaxy was promised a new age of peace and security. Many believed the promise, memorably delivered by the freshly self-appointed Emperor Palpatine, to cheers from a war-weary senate. Recordings of that declaration echoed across the HoloNet. At long last, the Clone Wars were over, and the mistakes that led to that scourge would not be repeated. There would be order forged from chaos. While framed as a political promise of military strength, it was understood, if not explicitly said, that such order would extend to criminal justice.

The Empire had at its disposal new warships, new soldiers, and new combat equipment from now conquered battlefields. These displays of military might became soaring symbols of patriotism. To love the Empire was to love the stormtrooper, the TIE fighter, and the Star Destroyer. Symbols of local law enforcement were afterthoughts, and cops were largely assumed to be an extension of the military.

Per the bureaucratic definition, the two were separate entities—but in practice, the lines were blurred. Some of the best police candidates were funneled into the Imperial war machine, leaving local departments understaffed. Community patrols were replaced with sensor apparatus feeding centralized surveillance centers.

The Imperial government, obsessed with implementing a defined standard across a galaxy of variables, attempted to create a uniform Imperial legal code that would apply to the entire Empire and codify criminal offenses.

The revised Imperial penal code broke crime into five main categories of infraction:

- Class Five infractions were the least severe cases, such as failure to comply with license standards for ships, vehicles, or equipment or nonlethal incidents of public disturbances. Punishment typically consisted of a small fine of up to 1,000 credits.
- Class Four infractions included the purchase, possession, and/or transportation of contraband other than weaponry, as well as the transport of certain goods without Imperial tariffs or permits. Aggravated, nonlethal assault also registered as a Class Four infraction. Punishment could include a fine up to 5,000 credits and some jail time.
- Class Three infractions included aiding and abetting known

felons, grand theft, and the attempted bribing of Imperial officials. Punishment involved the suspension of piloting licenses, upwards of 5,000-credit fines, and jail time.
- Class Two infractions included murder; manslaughter; major fraud or embezzlement; assaults on law enforcement; purchase or transportation of stolen goods; sale or transport of weaponry without a permit. Punishment could be fines upwards of 10,000 credits and significant jail time (up to thirty standard years).
- Class One infractions included conspiracy against the Empire and violence against the Imperial military, piracy or other attacks against a starship, or aiding and abetting acts of terrorism/rebellion. Punishment could include arrest or summary execution.

The Empire may have codified the law, but it gave alarming freedom to the police officers to interpret the situation. Rewards tied to quotas regarding the routing of traitors or conspirators led to cops inflating charges and carrying out judgment on their own. When many crimes or criminals of the time operated in gray areas, the penal code reduced the law to black and white—with offenses falling more often in the black.

Because the Galactic Empire demanded results in cracking down on rebellion, planetary police forces were compelled to serve the demands of the Imperial Security Bureau or Imperial Intelligence. The rise of the rebellion led some planets to enact martial law. Local law enforcement would then be eclipsed by military law, with stormtroopers becoming the norm on city streets.

In this complicated era, my mother, Andressa Divo, graduated from a law enforcement academy, becoming an inspector. She was devoted to justice, but also believed deeply in the promises of the Emperor. She was among the deceived. This is not meant to absolve her from the complicity in some of the questionable things required of her by the Empire. Her case files instead demonstrate her devotion to duty and belief in the laws, regardless of the government that wrote them. The files also highlight the fact that many of the civil injustices of the government extended to the criminal world. The unforgiving penal code left some lawful citizens with no choice but lawless acts of treason, while the military bureaucracy created loopholes that allowed true criminals to seep deeper into the shadows.

FILE / 7965.211.0

ANDRESSA DIVO, ISB RALLY

Tan Divo retired with honors within the early years of the Empire. His daughter, Andressa, was eager to continue the family tradition of service, and enrolled in the same academy as her father. Upon graduation, however, a new avenue was available to Andressa that was not to her father: the Imperial Security Bureau.

The ISB grew out of policing efforts during the fragmented age of the Clone Wars to seek out sedition, Separatist collaboration, and crimes of treason against the Republic. Loyalty toward order and authority were paramount in this time of dissension, and the ISB used the growing military intelligence apparatus to quickly become a powerful law enforcement agency with a sweeping scope and presence.

Andressa Divo saw the toll the Clone Wars took on both the galaxy and her father. She absorbed the speeches of Palpatine and his cabinet, and enthusiastically welcomed the coming of the Empire. She had her eyes set on the ISB during her academy days, and rose through its ranks quickly. The power vacuum that followed the destruction of the first Death Star and the death of so many bureau chiefs, and the Empire's focus on rooting out rebellion, was an accelerant to her career. As the Empire's military state grew more and more powerful, so too did Agent Andressa Divo.

She kept in correspondence with her father as her agent duties transported her off Coruscant to scattered theaters of operation. Her notes as well as Tan Divo's marginalia supplement the visuals in this chapter.

ISB PATROL: INTAKE OF PRISONERS ON CORUSCANT

If Republic law enforcement and bounty hunters made for strange bedfellows, it was all the more stranger for the Empire. Bounty hunters became an expeditious means to an end. Used to help capture fugitives who had fled to the barrens of the Outer Rim Territories, bounty hunters were indicative of Imperial shortcomings, so their use was not to be loudly touted by the Empire. The upper echelons of the Imperial military disparaged the use of bounty hunters, thinking it beneath the proud traditions of law enforcement and order. But it was rumored (though never conclusively proven) that the office of the Emperor and his emissaries had private accounts with bounty hunter guilds to carry out extrajudicial captures kept far from the official Imperial record. Agent Divo kept a growing file of potential bounty hunters for Imperial use. From her correspondence with her father:

Father, it may interest you to know that the name Boba Fett crossed my docket today. I know you had kept an eye on him early in his career. He answered the call of remandation for Isquik Tors (remember him?), Quarren pirate of Lamaredd. It was an unexpected welcome delivery, and Fett said few words, despite hauling the perp all the way to our landing pad on the capital.

SCRUMRATS ATTACK SURVEILLANCE CAM

To facilitate the military expansion of the Empire, the shipyards throughout the Core and Inner Rim were nationalized, including the famed production facilities of Corellia. When such industrial titans as Kuat Drive Yards and Sienar Fleet Systems tried to pin their missed quotas on acts of sabotage, the Imperial Security Bureau investigated such claims.

Partnering with the local Corellian Security Forces (CorSec), an ISB inspection team led by Agent Divo scoured the impoverished favelas that surrounded the sprawling industrial sites, attempting to find evidence to corroborate these claims. Reports spoke of a Lady Proxima being the head of a gang called the White Worms who "owned" the turf closest to the Coronet spaceport and the adjacent factories. Agent Divo wrote:

We spelunked the darkest sewers that would give the Coruscant undercity lessons in wretchedness, while other agents audited the claims of KDY and SFS execs. Our probes found criminals all right— street urchins known as Scrumrats. But their crimes were little more than petty theft and pickpocketing.

These territorial whelps destroyed our probe, so add property damage to their tracsheet.

The execs were shuffling blame down the social ladder, not thinking we'd bother taking a closer look. We did find minor evidence of power taps that drew from factory generators to warm the Scrumrat tunnels, but nothing that would account for their production losses. It would seem it's the executives that have some explaining to do, not these children.

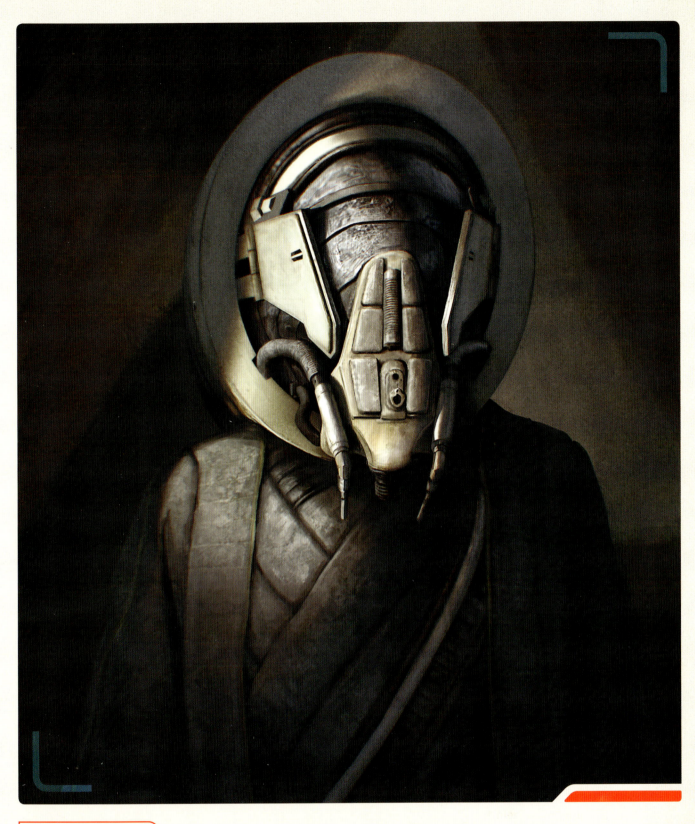

FILE / 7966.781.1

MOLOCH OF THE WHITE WORMS HOLO

The ISB investigation never found a trace of Lady Proxima in the mazelike warrens beneath the Coronet favelas, but Agent Divo's report listed her as a Grindalid, a light-sensitive species of annelids. The species gave the gang its name, but it appeared the principal operatives of the organization were mostly subadult humans and humanoids.

The closest the ISB was able to come to the leader of the White Worms was a Grindalid known only as Moloch. A proper holo of his countenance was not possible as he refused to remove his mask due to his photosensitivity. Local authorities had encountered Moloch before, but his criminal record was marked with only warnings and fines after incidents of altercations and violence. Agent Divo wrote:

Upon inspection of White Worm activity, none of this appears politically motivated. Yes, there were minor infractions to be policed, but the theft of ergs, the intimidation of off-hour factory workers, and the fleecing of tourists is a matter for CorSec, not ISB.

STREET RACING SURVEILLANCE IMAGE

During her investigation into the favelas of Corellia, Agent Divo began amassing a file on illegal street racing, based on reports gathered by CorSec. Her rationale was that a leniency in laws that allowed such activity was a harbinger of greater corruption and perhaps the mark of larger organized crime. In correspondence with her father, Tan Divo, she wrote:

Father, I recalled your work creating a case to keep podracing off Coruscant. It appears Corellia could have used your diligence. The poorest neighborhoods in Coronet and Tyrena support a race circuit that brings in hard-earned credits through crooked gambling. Nowhere near as sophisticated as the podrace racket, it nonetheless shows initiative and organization that surprised me. Imagine if these energies were funneled to useful, lawful endeavors!

The White Worms did have some connection to the racing, sponsoring entrants or offering supplies and technical assistance at a cost to racers. As it became clear the racing was not connected to any seditious acts, Agent Divo left it to CorSec to settle.

58

FILE / 7966.045.2

STOLEN ARTIFACTS

Collating theft reports from a variety of small museums in the Mid and Outer Rim revealed a pattern that points to Dryden Vos, capo of the Crimson Dawn syndicate. Some artifacts were taken by force, while others were acquired by bribing security or museum officials. Though the Imperial Security Bureau did not set foot in Dryden Vos' private study aboard his yacht *First Light*, it was known he had a collection of antiquities on display that may or may not contain these items. Especially frustrating was the evidence that Vos knew, entertained, and befriended Imperial officials, none of whom stepped forward with any word against Vos or his actions.

Stolen items presumed in Vos's collection:

1. From the Museum of Mythos on Kalavela, a nearly full suit of Mandalorian rally master armor vanished. Rally masters served as battlefield commanders during the ancient wars of Mandalorian expansion that helped define their current territorial borders.

2. From the Antiquities Institute of the Tion Hegemony, the ou'tranoi, a sacred vase said to collect the souls of enemies by the shamans of Golus Pheyar. Review of the holographic security footage at the Institute showed Hylobon mercenaries carrying out the deed. Vos was known to employ such beings as enforcers.

3. From the Private Collection of Barpotomous Drebble (who insisted he obtained it legally prior to its unsolved theft), a Godoan artifact known as the Dancing Goddess, of great spiritual import to the Godoans.

FILE / 7966.045.2

STOLEN ARTIFACTS (CONTINUED)

4. The Archaic Arsenal of Ordo and Scabbard Monument of Krownest each claimed losses of ancient Mandalorian weapons within weeks of each other—a rally master lance and a munit'kad halberd. For a time, both worlds suspected each other for the theft. The irony was if Vos did indeed have these in his collection, along with the rally master armor, he brought together related artifacts that Mandalorians have been unable to for centuries.

5. Snatched from the Royal Durosian Gallery this armillery sphere detailing the ancient Core Worlds and navigable routes, that denote the ancient alignment of Duros, Alderaan and Corellia, was considered by scholars to be the cradle of galactic civilization.

6. The Bureau of Ships and Services Heritage Museum on Coruscant reported the theft (and replacement with a forgery) of an ancient navigational dataplaque said to be from an old Jedi survey craft, the Permondiri Explorer. Aside from the storage rods built into its precious metal capacitance board, the plaque was adorned with traditional symbols denoting light, dark and the balance in between.

ZOOM 15 X

FILE / 7971.325.3

HONDO OHNAKA SECURITY IMAGE

A report from Trammis III spotted Hondo Ohnaka at the Chreotan Souk, selling contraband puffer pig bladders and Sansanna preservatives. Ohnaka's tracsheet of crimes had expanded during the time of Empire beyond the capital crimes of armed piracy, kidnapping, and extortion. ISB reports gathered by Agent Alexsandr Kallus implicated Ohnaka in a number of seditious plots undertaken by known rebel collaborators. The Imperial Office of Criminal Investigation (IOCI) placed an official Notice of Imperial Remandation on Ohnaka with Regional Classification throughout the Outer Rim and a bounty of 25,000 credits, with a 20,000-credit bonus for information leading to the arrest of Ohnaka's confederates, pending approval by Governor Ahrinda Pryce of Lothal.

The IOCI datacore posting had comments from the open community including ones whose origin signature pointed to Trammis III:

Good luck, my friends! If I can in any way help with the capture of so dashing and handsome a pirate king, perhaps we can split the bounty! Who wants to partner up?

Experts believe this was Ohnaka himself.

FILE / 7970.882.4

SEIZED COUNTERFEIT CREDITS

As the Republic transformed into the Empire, to stave off acts of counterfeiting and bolster confidence in galactic currency, the Empire did not supplant the countless physical Republic credits already in circulation. Electronic credits were seamlessly transformed into the new Galactic Imperial Credit Standard. Confederacy money was outlawed, wiping out stockpiles of wealth accumulated during the Clone Wars.

Physical credits predominantly drew their value from the treasury of the Empire, but they did have an inherent value for those not directly connected to the Imperial economy. Physical ingots had traces of aurodium, a precious metal, mixed with baser synthetics. There was less aurodium in a credit ingot than its face value, but credits could be melted down and distilled to their aurodium core for those looking for a currency more "real." The aurodium existed not only to give a physical value, but to limit unauthorized replication, as aurodium was expensive and cannot be duplicated. Forgers tried, however, and false ingots of valueless material spilled out of the furnaces of skilled counterfeiters. A dusting of pyrodium fooled cursory examination, both by eye or by electronics, but a concerted scan would reveal the forgery. Forgery of Imperial credits was a Class Two infraction, and could result in a sector bounty posting of 3,000 to 50,000 credits, depending on the denominations involved.

66

FILE / 7976.131.1

MALKITE POISONER GEAR

There are criminal organizations in the galaxy that justify their existence by pointing to history. They have existed, in one form or another, for centuries, and they feel such tradition warrants their continuation. The Malkite poisoners, a secret society of assassins, have been in operation for millennia. Their lore became enmeshed with conspiracy tales and galactic popular culture to the point

that it's difficult to extricate fact from fiction. It's been joked that every unsolved murder of the past thousand years has been the result of a Malkite poisoner, lurking in the shadows.

After the death of Admiral Jyrom Ottdell from zolall extract, Agent Divo began an investigation of the Malkite poisoners, which led her to some dark pockets of the HoloNet. She made several remote contacts with anonymous

beings, and was able to order, at great expense, several "Malkite poisoner kits," as they were advertised. Of the two dozen she received from different sources, all but one were fake and worthless, clearly the result of Holonet scam artists. But one kit came with an ampule of rare zolall poison, and inscribed on the dosage label were the cryptic words, *"Give it up, Agent, and watch what you drink."*

FILE / 7972.113.2

SINRICH HOLOGRAPHIC CLOAKING UNIT

An attempt to steal artifacts from the Imperial Museum on Coruscant led ISB to net the would-be thieves, who were equipped with exotic technology. Small holographic projectors with high-powered analyzer and emitter nodes rendered the thieves practically invisible; in effect, they were personal cloaking devices. Agent Divo's analysis of this case benefited from an investigation her father handled during the Clone Wars—a case that dealt with a Jedi-thwarted assassination attempt on Chancellor Palpatine. The plot hinged on the use of small holographic disguise matrix emitters, developed by the technical genius and artist from Cadomai, Sinrich. A comparison of the newer devices with the matrices confiscated during the Clone Wars showed a direct evolution of the technology, though Sinrich himself had vanished during the Clone Wars and was believed dead. From Agent Divo's notes:

Someone is building onto Sinrich's work if not Sinrich himself. The concept is simple but the technology complex. A holographic shield envelops the subject, and uses lensing techniques to wrap imagery from behind the subject to the front of it, making it look invisible with minimal distortion. This wrapping extends beyond the visible spectrum and is effective against infrared and ultraviolet wavelengths as well.

Agent Divo turned this evidence over to Imperial Intelligence, whose weapons divisions examined it closely for possible replication.

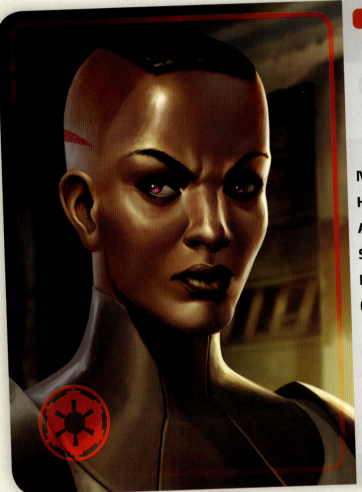

IMPERIAL
PEACEKEEPING
CERTIFICATE

NAME: KETSU ONYO

HOMEWORLD: SHUKUT, MANDALORIAN CITIZENSHIP

AGE: 18 STANDARD YEARS

SEX: FEMALE

HEIGHT: 1.78 METERS

CERTIFICATE NUMBER: 935913636/.M331

SIGNATURE/MARK:

ANY ATTEMPT TO ALTER PUNISHABLE BY DEATH. IMPERIAL OFFICE OF CRIMINAL INVESTIGATION

FILE / 7973.121.0

BOUNTY HUNTER PROFILE: KETSU ONYO

Among those on Agent Divo's bounty hunter shortlist was Ketsu Onyo, a former cadet at the Imperial Academy on Mandalore who dropped out of school and pursued a career as a hunter. According to official reports, she was a security retainer for XTS transport, which, according to Divo's notes, translated into hired gun for the Black Sun syndicate. Holographic imagery of Onyo speaking before the XTS board, made up of suspected Black Sun gangsters, does nothing to dispel Agent Divo's hypothesis.

While Agent Divo took care to annotate that Onyo did not make the cut on her preferred hunter list, she did later forward her notes to ISB Agent Alexsandr Kallus with the following addendum:

Kallus, this may be of interest to you. I had researched hunter Onyo for an aborted project, but her files point to a shared background with your quarry, Sabine Wren. From my analysis, Onyo is a capable pilot and warrior, well-equipped and well-funded, with a clean record as far as Imperial law is concerned. Whether or not she would turn on Wren is for your expertise to determine. Happy hunting.

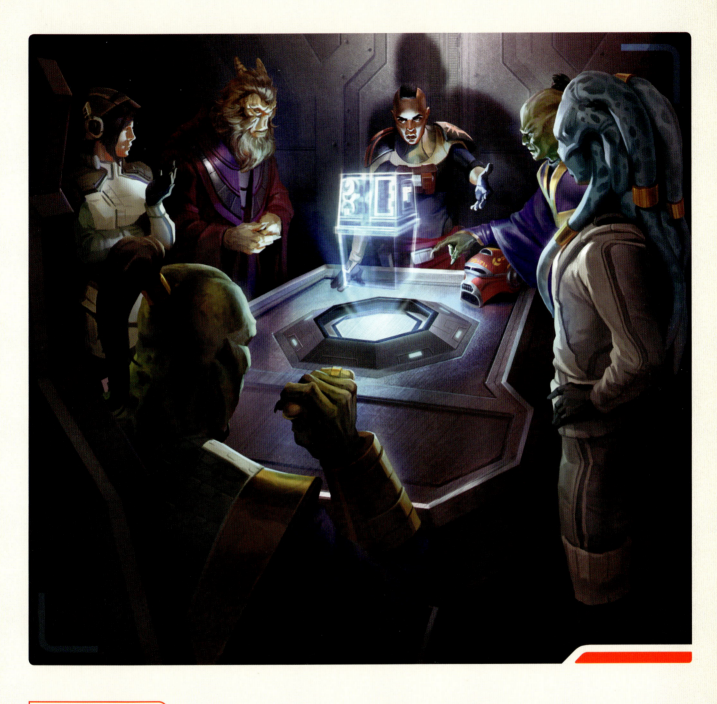

FILE / 7973.120.7

KETSU ONYO AND BLACK SUN SECURITY IMAGE

An undated soundless security image of Ketsu Onyo meeting with the XTS executive board—commonly thought to be the Black Sun leadership—was believed to capture her resignation. Though her temperamental departure risked making an enemy of the cartel, it appears she suffered no reprisal. A public record search on her security contract shows she carried out her employment to the letter, and left open the possibility of future consultant work.

Agent Divo wrote:

If we would ever need to infiltrate Black Sun, I can think of few candidates better than Ketsu Onyo. Her independence would mean not having to feign deep loyalty to the cartel, but her skill has earned her their respect.

Divo's files go on to propose a plan for utilizing bounty hunters of this type as intelligence agents, but Colonel Wulff Yularen of the ISB rejected it outright. He wrote:

We cannot expect reliable intelligence to come from someone willing to work for the highest bidder. That their loyalty is up for sale to begin with should tell you all you need to know about this scum.

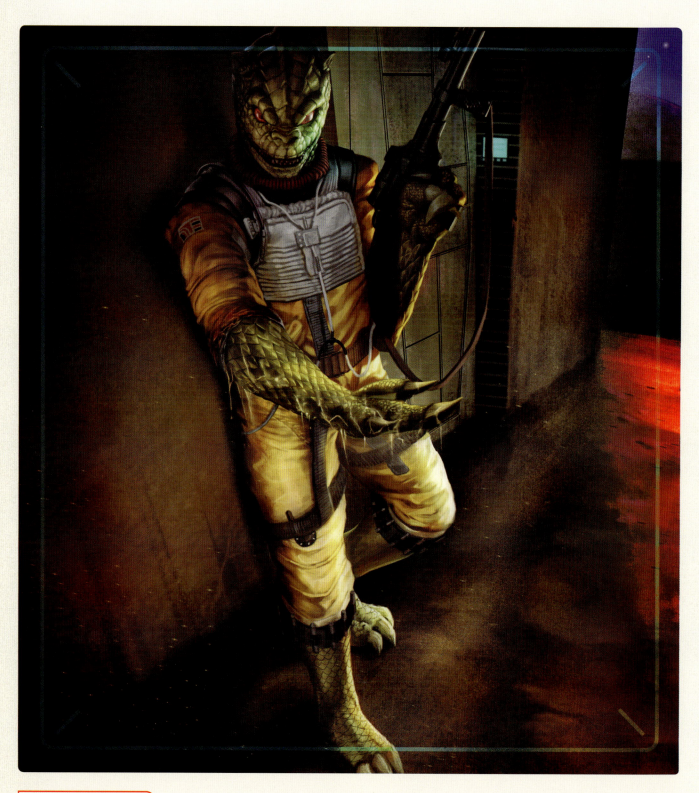

FILE / 7973.224.1

BOSSK AND BOSSK'S REMAINS (CAS334DD)

Also in Agent Divo's dossier, marked with "proceed to shortlist" was a copy of Bossk's Imperial Peacekeeping Certificate (IPKC) and other attachments related to his long and storied career. The Trandoshan hunter was active before the Clone Wars, and was instrumental in cowing the Wookiee uprising that followed the pacification of Kashyyyk at the war's end. A known associate of Boba Fett and founding member of the Krayt's Claw posse, Bossk eventually returned to operating on his own when that group was disbanded. Bossk travels the spacelanes in a modified YV-666 freighter called the *Hound's Tooth*. From Agent Divo's notes:

Bossk's criminal record was expunged with the coming of the Empire, but he no doubt continues to operate in the criminal fringe, especially in Hutt Space. As far as Imperial warrants go, he has scored twelve captures, eight of them alive.

FILE / 7973.224.1

BOSSK AND BOSSK'S REMAINS (CONTINUED)

Appended to Bossk's profile were evidence records (CAS334DD) taken from an ill-fated attempt to stop a Wookiee berserker on Ord Mantell. From Agent Divo's notes:

Trandoshans are a hardy lot. The preserved jar holds a torn arm from a Trandoshan male, ripped off cleanly by an enraged Wookiee. Analysis with shed skin samples from Bossk's domicile confirmed a match. He's since regenerated that arm. Looks like the old lizard can take more than a punch and return to the fight.

FILE / 7976.611.3

BOBA FETT AND FETT GEAR ANALYSIS

Agent Divo took a different kind of interest in Boba Fett than her father did. Though the elder Divo showed sympathy for a child robbed of a childhood by the circumstances of the Clone Wars, the ISB agent instead showed analytic admiration for Fett's record. *"They've lost count of his captures,"* she annotates. *"Very few of them were alive."*

Agent Divo's research included files on Jango Fett's career, with highlighted similarities between father's and son's reputations. With the coming of the Empire, Boba Fett was able to cement his reputation as bounty hunter in the Outer Rim Territories, avoiding the Core Worlds unless the price made it worth his risk. Like Bossk, he was one of a handful of bounty hunters with Republic criminal records who were effectively pardoned by the government to free up the use of capable independent law enforcers in the Outer Rim. Agent Divo writes:

This is not corroborated, but the judicial officer who tried to proffer the pardon to Fett was initially rebuffed. His heavily redacted account of the situation says that Fett didn't respond to "charity" and had no interest in being "indebted" to the Empire.

Exactly what settled the matter between Fett and the Empire was not

FILE / 7976.611.3

BOBA FETT AND FETT GEAR ANALYSIS (CONTINUED)

in the records, but Agent Divo noted that as of her tenure in the Imperial Security Bureau, Fett was not only on an Imperial retainer but came with highly placed—and highly classified—recommendations.

Also in Agent Divo's notes was a description of the gear that Fett was most infamously known for.

There is no shortage of knockoff Mandalorian gear in circulation among

the bounty hunting profession, with remolded and painted plastoid trying to pass off as genuine beskar. I believe Fett's equipment to be authentic, even though he is not of Mandalorian heritage. Inventory records and comparative analysis shows Fett to be sporting an authentic Mitrinomon Transports Z-6 jetpack and gauntlets with Mando-designed dart launchers, flame projectors, and concealed blades.

74

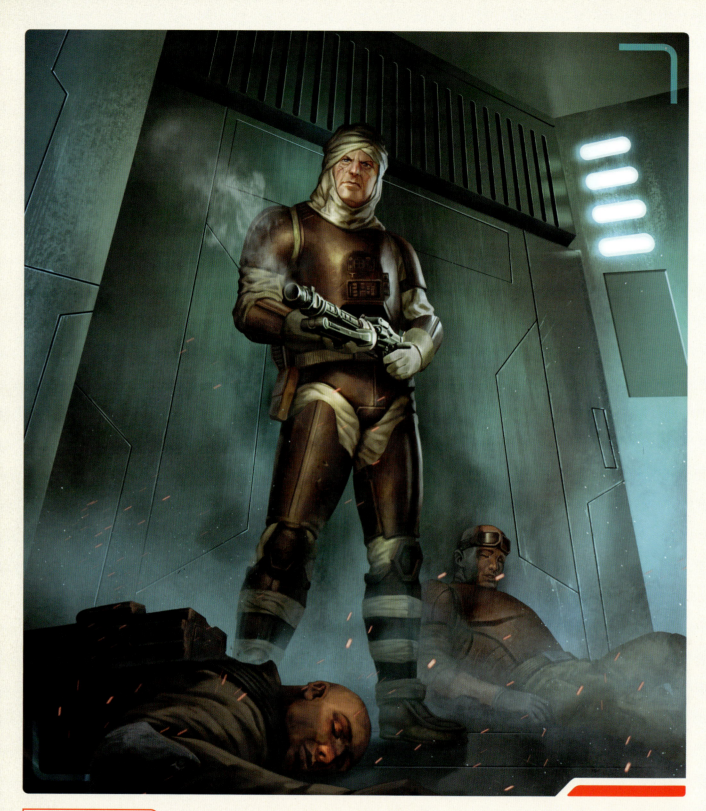

DENGAR AND DENGAR GEAR ANALYSIS

Known by no name other than Dengar, this Corellian bounty hunter had a career that peaked during the Clone Wars. He was known to be a sometime associate of the Krayt's Claw posse. He disappeared from circulation for a brief time at war's end, believed to have been recuperating from a near-fatal injury. Images of him taken after he resurfaced confirm a more haggard and grizzled appearance. In his youth as a gladiator, Dengar was spry and capable of nimble unarmed combat, but during the age of Empire, his aching body favored long-range combat or more brutish fisticuffs. As Agent Divo wrote:

His headdress may be a traditional Agrilatian turban, but it's little wonder people mistake it for bandaging as Dengar's taciturn nature and plodding style resembles someone who has suffered head trauma. Despite his inarticulate manner, he does get results and specializes in heavy gear and explosives. His Imperial record: twenty-three captures, six alive. That's the ratio of an imprecise but effective man.

A close examination of Dengar's preferred gear (see image on the right) reveals it to consist of Imperial surplus armor. He has never explained its origins.

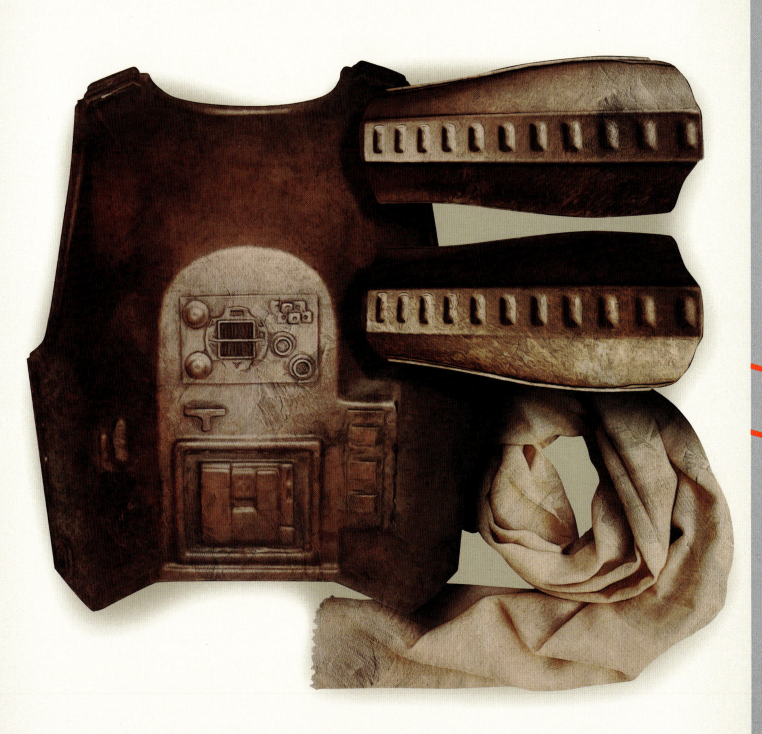

FILE / 7979.231.4

IG-88 (AKA PHLUTDROID)

The IG-series of combat automata saw its zenith during the Clone Wars, where Banking Clan-backed Separatists unleashed phalanxes of these chrome war droids onto the battlefield. After the defeat of the Separatists, the conquered war droids were destined to be scrapped at junkyards across the galaxy, but the liberation efforts of the Droid Gotra spared many droids this fate. It is believed that IG-88 was liberated by the Gotra, but refused membership to the organization, preferring to remain independent. It was illegal for the droid to acquire an IPKC license, so IG-88 was essentially an unlicensed bounty hunter. Nonetheless, it carved out a career hunting escaped fugitives in the Outer Rim Territories. Agent Divo had a case file on IG-88, with a recommendation for further investigation. Her father did not take this lightly, as his correspondence noted:

I cannot believe the Empire would countenance the usage of such machines. Didn't we fight a war to stop such armies of killers? I strongly disagree with treating this thing as anything but a weapon, Andressa. This is not a police droid. This is an uninhibited murderer with no sense of value for life or order. Nothing good will come of it.

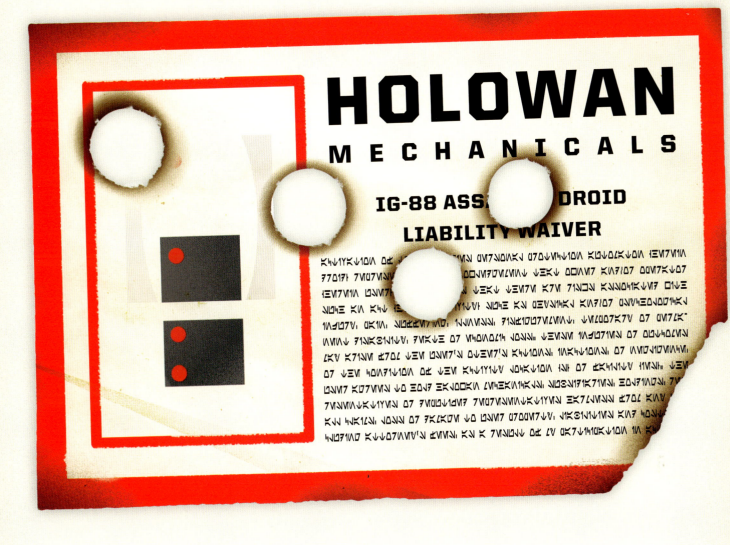

HOLOWAN
MECHANICALS

IG-88 ASSA███ DROID
LIABILITY WAIVER

FILE / 7979.231.3

HOLOWAN MECHANICALS EUA WAIVER

After the Clone Wars, wherein combat automata manufactured by Holowan Mechanicals resulted in untold death and damage, many expected the corporation to face severe censure if not outright dismantling for its role in arming Separatist forces. While Holowan lobbyists and lawyers prevented the company from facing meaningful reprisals, changes in the legal code made battle droids illegal. Holowan found ways of getting its most profitable product to deep-pocketed clientele by repositioning their military hardware as personal protection droids, a cynical bureaucratic distinction that did not make the weapons any less deadly.

As part of the legally ironclad user agreement, purchasers of the Holowan Mechanicals IG-series waived the company of any liabilities resulting from injury, death, or damage from the droid. The IG-series was notoriously prone to violent personality glitches if subjected to third-party or aftermarket modifications. This was an example of where the power wielded by megacorporations in the Empire far outweighed interest in public safety, and there was nothing those in law enforcement could do to even out the scales.

ZUCKUSS AND GAND GEAR ANALYSIS

Operation outside the bounds of Imperial procedure led to the growth of eccentricities that would find no place within the ISB. Case in point: the bounty hunter Zuckuss, a findsman in the ancient Gand tradition. Zuckuss was a storied bounty hunter, but it was his methodology that attracted attention rather than his effectiveness (which was nonetheless admirable). In short, Zuckuss spooked even hardened hunters with his reliance on the spiri-tual. An early exam- ination by the Inquisitorius confirmed that Zuckuss did not register on whatever they used to measure capability in the Force, but the Gand nonetheless used extra-sensory abilities beyond the scope of modern Imperial science. Agent Divo wrote:

I am not a superstitious person, but there is an unshakable, ghostly sense that creeps into my periphery when I am witness to a Gand findsman undertaking his ritual. With Zuckuss's agreement, we holographically recorded his meditation with his braziers and sensing herbs, his chanting and poses, and witnessed as he tracked down a deliberately hidden target in the span of mere minutes. Imperial scientists posit that the Gand physiology is operating in spectra undetectable to us humans and our instrumentation, but it is hard to dismiss the idea that something else is afoot.

The scattered, isolated colonies of Gand on their mist-shrouded world has led to the findsman culture varying in custom and trappings. There has not been deep cultural study as the Gand are a reclusive folk. Zuckuss is a Laromun'rac follower, a denomination of faith native to the Osia'Kru Brume lowlands. His findsman ceremonies center on the burning of altasocra sage in an ancient kanger bowl. When time is short, he employs a prac- tical and modern evolution of the ritual with electrically heated resin tubes affixed to his breather helmet. The interaction of the resin vapor with the compound receptors of his insectoid eyes shift his vision deeper into the ultraviolet and infrared spectra, giving him enhanced perception and visual acuity.

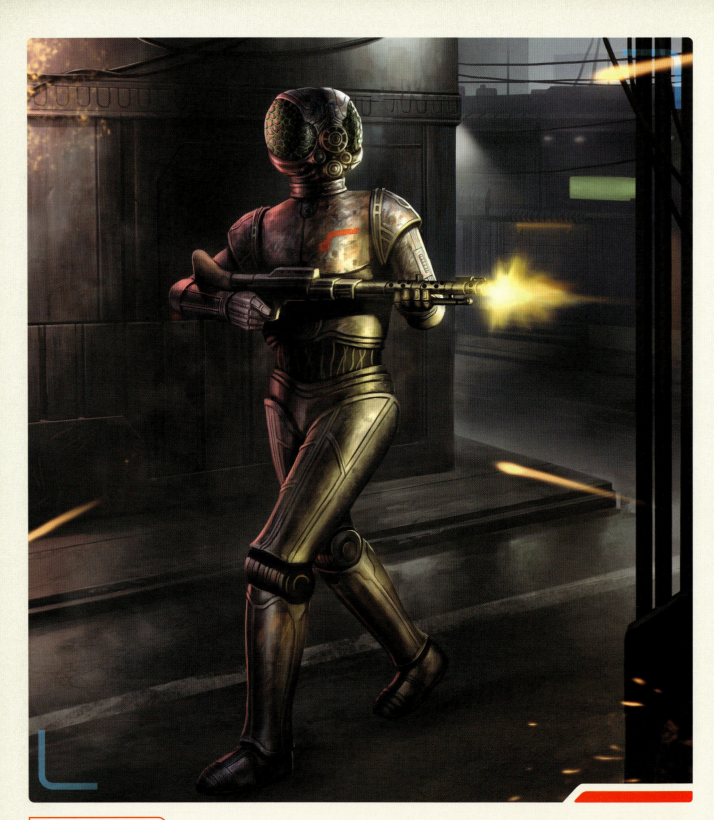

FILE / 7979.313.3

4-LOM AND 4-LOM HISTORY ANALYSIS

Another unusual bounty-hunting candidate was 4-LOM, what appeared to be a LOM-series protocol droid that had manumitted itself for independent operation as a bounty hunter. The pivot from protocol droid to hired gun was so extreme that Industrial Automaton, manufacturer of the LOM, spent a great deal of credits to bury stories about 4-LOM and prevent the general public from knowing these droids could

become killers due to a software flaw. Slicer droids affiliated with the Droid Gotra nevertheless spread the word about 4-LOM, holding the bounty hunter droid as a shining example of how function does not determine future, as per their abolitionist rhetoric. Agent Divo noted:

I was fascinated with the case of 4-LOM just for the sheer unlikelihood

of this droid's transformation. Given the Droid Gotra's zeal for promoting 4-LOM's story, it's my hypothesis that they were the originators of the malignant programming that corrupted the droid. Research through captured Droid Gotra databanks unveiled a campaign to target the Kuari Princess, a luxury liner. I, like many in the ISB, first assumed it was to be the target of

...laxing in elegant comfort. With the press of a beckon... ...our expertly programmed cabin steward droids... ...end to your needs, and leave your stateroom... ...eccable shape. These droids are available in... ...variety of morphologies to make any species... ...me. Simply press D17 on the in-room control... ...he steward right for you.

FILE / 7979.313.3

4-LOM AND 4-LOM HISTORY ANALYSIS (CONTINUED)

piracy, and when no such attack by the Gotra took place, it was largely forgotten. It was not until a review of *Kuari Princess* brochures that a possible explanation occurred to me. Promotional imagery (see evidence fragment above) included a view of the *Kuari Princess's* wide array of droid cabin stewards, in various shapes and sizes meant to accommodate guests of different backgrounds. Among them was a LOM unit in *Kuari Princess* livery. Although I cannot prove it, it is my belief that the Gotra targeted the Princess with the intent of freeing 4-LOM to be a droid enforcer in their ranks.

FILE / 7980.111.1

BOUNTY HUNTER TOOLS OF THE TRADE

The Imperial Peacekeeping Certificate, simply known as a bounty hunters' license, is a permit to carry a wide assortment of weaponry that would otherwise be considered illegal for private citizens to wield. In theory, the IPKC is only issued to applicants who produce accredited weapons and demonstrate safety training. In practice, the process is expedited with rush fees that bypass the jams of Imperial bureaucracy. As such, the bounty hunter trade is filled with unqualified but affluent adventure seekers, who often fall into the familiar habit of copying what works. From Agent Divo's notes:

For every experienced and effective bounty hunter, there are a dozen rich wannabes, thinking they'll be the next Boba Fett or Black Krrsantan as long as they look the part. I've lost track of how many times we've scraped the blasted remains of a weekend hunter off the permacrete and found him packing a knock-off EE-3 carbine rifle or plastoid Mando armor.

This collection of recovered weaponry was annotated by Divo to note the more famous hunters and criminals these items were likely meant to emulate, from the anti-security blades and sonic beam weapons used by Boba Fett and the DL-21 blaster favored by Ponda Baba to a thermal detonator of the type customized by Puggles Trodd and the GRS-1 snare rifle made famous by Zuckuss.

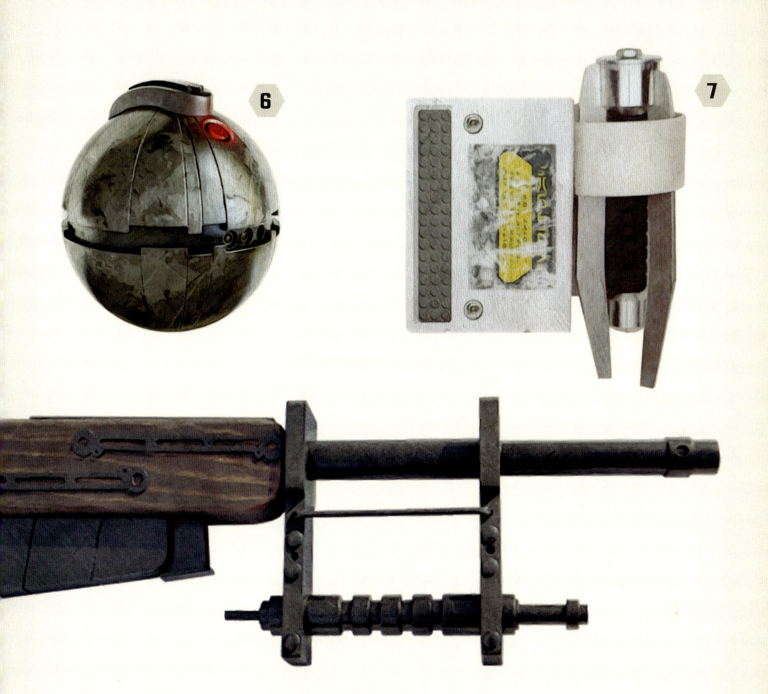

6

7

LEGEND

1. BlasTech DL-21 blaster pistol with heat dissipation vanes on muzzle

2. Specialized blaster reactant gas ampules

3. GRS-1 snare rifle with integral liquid cable launch reservoir

4. Sonic pulse generator

5. Monomolecular and electro-ribbon anti-security blade

6. Customized Merr-Sonn Munitions thermal detonator

7. Stormtrooper-issue grapnel and syntherope spool

ᐱᐤᐃᗰᐱ NOTICE ||||　　　BY IMPERIAL DECREE ALL CITIZENS MUST SUBMIT ANY INFORMATION REGARDING REBEL INSURGENTS

WANTED

FOR CRIMES AGAINST THE EMPIRE

SAW GERRERA

FOR MURDER, TERRORISM, TREASON

HEIGHT: 1.87M

GENDER: MALE

SPECIES: HUMAN

AGE: UNKNOWN

SHOULD BE CONSIDERED ARMED AND DANGEROUS. USE CAUTION.

The Empire is seeking the capture, or positive proof of death, of known rebel leader

Known Associates: Beezer Fortuna, Moroff, Weeteef Cyu-Bee, Tognath eggmates Benthic "Two Tubes" and Edrio "Two Tubes"

It is the will of Emperor Palpatine to ensure the future of a stable and prosperous galaxy

FILE / 7971.020.9

WANTED: SAW GERRERA

The most serious and treasonous crimes in the Empire warranted the issuing of a "most wanted" bounty, with jurisdictional effect spreading across the entire galaxy. During the height of the Empire, only a few hundred individuals earned such notorious status. The status of most wanted could be issued by Grand Moffs, Grand Admirals, Grand Generals, and was subject to the Emperor's final approval. For years, Saw Gerrera was the most

wanted criminal in the galaxy. His rampant terrorist strikes resulted in atrocious civilian casualties earning him this distinction. He was known to subject prisoners to torture beyond the bounds of the Alderaan Convention. For years, the images of Gerrera and his partisans were used to drive recruitment into the Imperial military, as Gerrera was the worst of the rebels. The ISB benefited from using the reputation of Gerrera to encourage

citizens to report suspicious activity. From Agent Divo's notes:

Ask any ISB agent who their dream quarry is, they will tell you Saw Gerrera. I have spoken to Agent Kallus at length about the vicious nature of Gerrera's attacks, and he has shared details that give me such pause that I hesitate to record them here.

PRISONER:

HALLIK, LIANA

ᛂᚲᛃᛃᚻᛃ ᛃᚻᚲᛃᚲ

AGE:

22 SY (ESTIMATE)

SPECIES:

HUMAN

HEIGHT:

1.6 METERS

SITE OF ARREST:

CORULAG

FILE / 7976.994.5

LIANA HALLIK INTAKE HOLO

On occasion, the significance of an archival file does not become apparent until years after its original record date. After the fall of the Empire, New Republic Intelligence was given access to trillions of exanodes of Imperial files, which will take sifting droids years to fully examine. A Five Points Station arrest record of Lianna Hallik prior to her sentencing to the Wobani prison was flagged for further examination and directed to Mon Mothma for review. Mothma was able to confirm its authenticity as an alias used by Jyn Erso, leader of the doomed Rogue One mission that captured the Death Star plans early in the Galactic Civil War.

The arrest record was originally annotated by Imperial Admiral Bethava Rocwyn, of the Star Destroyer *Authority*, as follows:

Another petty criminal. Another stupid girl. Another piece of flotsam unable to find a place within the Empire other than as an obstacle to its glorious machinery. She at least has some spirit and a strong spine, so put her to work at one of the Emperor's labor camps, where we can wring some usage of her before she dries up and dies.

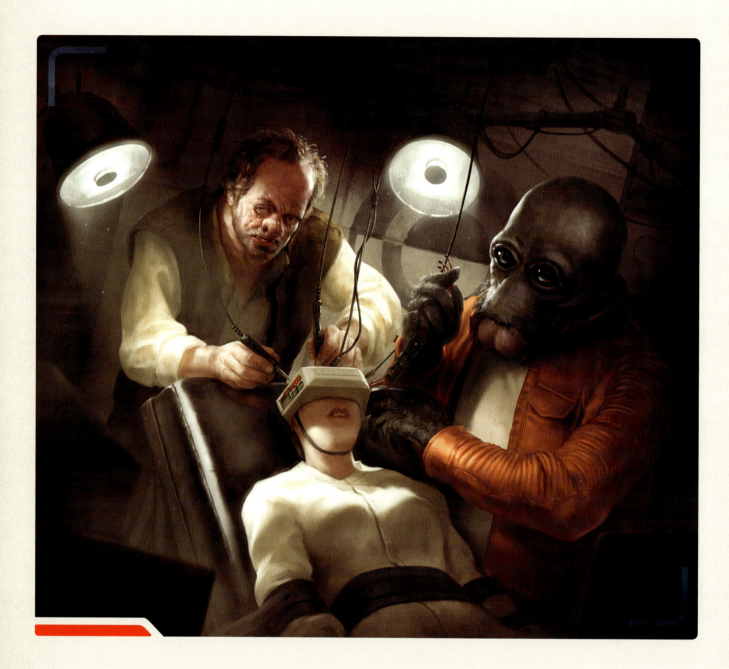

FILE / 7967.340.1

CORNELIUS EVAZAN SECURITY IMAGE AND CONCEPT EVIDENCE

Once a promising doctor from Alsakan, Cornelius Evazan exhibited socio-pathic tendencies while in the employ of Dryden Vos, a one-time leader in the Crimson Dawn syndicate. Evazan was Vos's personal doctor, on staff to monitor Vos's volatile physiology that was the result of a crossed heritage and past injuries. While in Vos's employ, Evazan satisfied his morbid curiosity in surgical experimentation, offering his services to modify underworld clients to disguise their identities or enhance their physical abilities. Once he had a taste for such

immoral modifications, he delved into even more ghastly experimentations, going so far as to create a surgically altered breed of subservient organics with droid sentience called the Decraniated. From Agent Divo:

Evazan's work is nothing short of a nightmare. His Decraniation process strips a subject of all free will, turning them into living droids carrying out the whims of their owners. It is a crime far worse than slavery, for at least slaves can be freed. The only freedom

that awaits the Decraniated is the release of death.

Evazan vanished after the death of Dryden Vos, potentially scared away by the changes within Crimson Dawn's command structure. His work, however, continued, with a rash of mutilations occurring in no less than a dozen star systems. The appearance of Decraniated on the battle-scarred streets of the moon of Jedha has led bounty hunters to assume he briefly operated there before moving on to parts unknown.

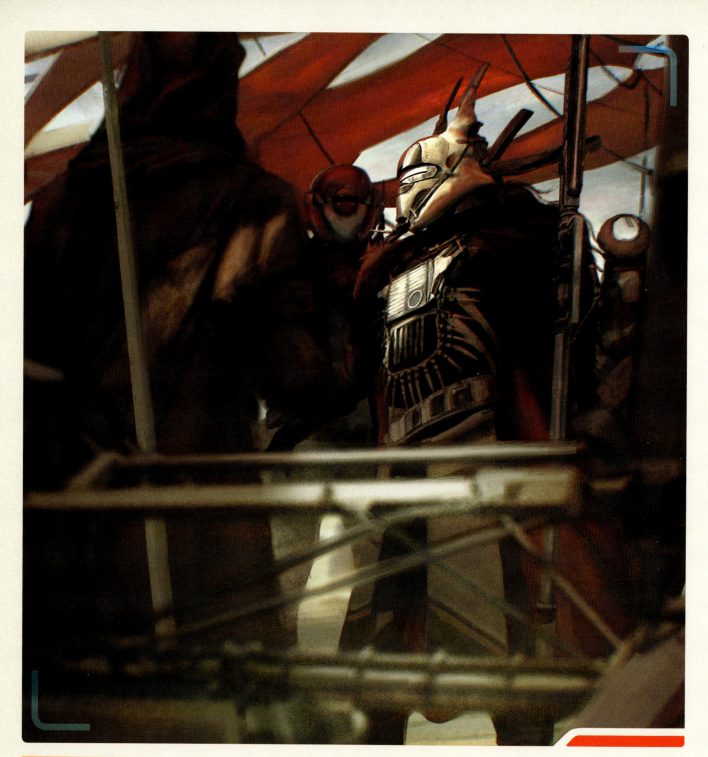

FILE / 7966.132.1

ENFYS NEST AND THE CLOUD-RIDERS SURVEILLANCE IMAGE

A rash of high-speed piracy in the Outer Rim led to the issuing of bounties on a mysterious marauder known as Enfys Nest. Arising in the Bheriz sector, Nest led the Cloud-Rider swoop gang. During the Empire's second decade, an increase in swoop gangs attracted thrill-seeking criminals with a disregard for safety, life, law, and property. They were extremely territorial, thus an overlap in swoop gang operations would inevitably lead to violent showdowns. For this reason, the Cloud-Riders stood out as being remarkably nomadic, concentrating their piracy on Imperial targets, or those affiliated with the Crimson Dawn syndicate. The lack of sophistication in approach and equipment led some to theorize they were a hired band, as they did not appear to capitalize much on the valuable cargoes they looted. Agent Divo had an alternate theory:

The consistency of the Cloud-Rider strikes makes me think they're not working for anyone, but rather are ideologically motivated. They keep their identities and numbers carefully hidden, and their strikes against Imperial targets are often timed for public spectacle as well as tactical efficiency. This may be the start of an insurrectionist movement, and should certainly be watched.

Holographic records gathered of Enfys Nest differ in details, leading Agent Divo to conclude Nest used decoys or imposters, in a Naboo royal-like gambit. Divo openly wondered whether or not there is in fact a singular being named Enfys Nest to give flesh and blood solidity to the growing legend.

FILE / 7966.212.0

EVIDENCE: CAPTURED CLOUD-RIDER SWOOP

A captured Incom Skyscythe v-132 belonging to a Cloud-Rider shows extensive overhauling of the repulsorlift yield cradle, with reinforced power-trunking distributing energy from an over-pressured turbo-ion accelerator, making for a very fast and very dangerous ride. The splayed steering vanes are reconfigured as a nod to starfighter S-foil assemblies- suggesting how exactly these Cloud-Riders envision their rides as air superiority combat craft. The foil-mounted airspeed indicators mimic the X-wing's laser cannons, in the same way some animals exhibit false patterns and colors to resemble predators—which distracts from this Skyscythe's true weapons, a pair of fixed cannons that draw power directly from the vehicle's engine block. The outrigger ion engines have independent power outputs, which increases the swoop's maneuverability. Extremely hard to control, an imbalance in the engine feeds can spin the craft around in a surprise 180-degree turn.

GARGON RAID HOLOCAM FOOTAGE

Observation holocam footage depicts a squad of Cloud-Rider marauders speeding from a target site. The object of their raid was an Imperial medical spice cache on Gargon. An analysis of the inventory of the raided cargo revealed that Nest took only the medicinally processed spice, segmented into ready-to-implement triage kits and emergency packs. The raw spice, the potentially more valuable cargo as it could be refined for narcotics usage, was left behind. Agent Divo noted:

My compatriots call this simply an anomaly, the result of a hurried grab of goods as our security forces closed in on Nest as the marauders. But it's clearly more than that. It would have been easier to grab the unrefined spice and make a fortune selling it. Nest is not in it for the money. I believe she's building an army and readying to go to war.

WANTED

FOR CRIMES AGAINST THE EMPIRE

BY IMPERIAL DECREE ALL CITIZENS MUST SUBMIT ANY INFORMATION REGARDING REBEL INSURGENTS

NOTICE ||||

BOM VIMDIN

HEIGHT: 1.8M

GENDER: MALE

SPECIES: ADVOZSE

AGE: 28 STANDARD YEARS

FOR COLLUSION, BRIBERY, THEFT, AND CONSPIRACY

It is the will of Emperor Palpatine to ensure the future of a stable and prosperous galaxy

FILE / 7977.44.3

WANTED: BOM VIMDIN

As the Empire extended its reach into formerly independent sectors of the Outer Rim, more and more assignments fell beyond the watchful gaze of loyalty officers of the Imperial Security Bureau. The distant outposts were oases of order surrounded by lawless deserts. Such difficult postings, far from the comforts of the Core, could tempt even the most loyal Imperials to break the law, and there were opportunists ready to offer such temptation. Bom Vimdin was one of the most successful Outer Rim smugglers and black marketeers. He had a keen eye for Imperials on the edge, and a willing-ness to risk contact with Imperial officials. Vimdin sold officers illicit sub-stances and entertainments not keeping within the codes of Imperial conduct. Agent Divo wrote:

While it is without question the

Imperial officials on the receiving end of a graft should be subject to the harshest response the ISB can muster, we cannot diminish the role that such tempters as Vimdin play. This Advozse is a disease-carrying parasite, against whom the Imperial immune system has yet to build a reliable defense— an amoral magnet that confuses the human moral compass.

ꡒꡍꡃꡒ NOTICE |||| BY IMPERIAL DECREE ALL CITIZENS MUST SUBMIT ANY INFORMATION REGARDING REBEL INSURGENTS

WANTED

FOR CRIMES AGAINST THE EMPIRE

CHELLI LONA APHRA

HEIGHT: 1.56M

GENDER: FEMALE

SPECIES: HUMAN

AGE: 24 STANDARD YEARS

FOR THEFT, FRAUD, DESTRUCTION OF IMPERIAL PROPERTY

It is the will of Emperor Palpatine to ensure the future of a stable and prosperous galaxy

---

FILE / 7977.934.1

WANTED: CHELLI LONA APHRA

Agent Divo compiled this case file at the request of Inspector Thanoth, an adjutant serving with Lord Darth Vader and investigating the theft of a large sum of credits being transported by an Imperial cruiser. While Divo was not given clearance to request more information regarding Thanoth's case, she was nonetheless thorough in her study of Chelli Lona Aphra, a disgraced archaeologist known to circle the criminal underworld. Though Thanoth valued succinct reports, Agent Divo over-delivered by attaching her personal assessment of Aphra, apparently in a bid to impress or curry favor with an Imperial so closely attached to Vader. An excerpt:

If I may, Inspector Thanoth, I cannot shake the conclusion that Dr. Aphra is but a small-scale operator, far beneath the notice of so esteemed a personage as Lord Vader. She is unlikely to achieve a notoriety beyond being an academic outcast. And although I am aware that Lord Vader values artifacts from a certain era, I am doubtful of Dr. Aphra's credentials and abilities to uncover anything of worth for his Lordship.

BAIL ORGANA AND MON MOTHMA SECURITY IMAGE

After Saw Gerrera, the next person on the most wanted list was Mon Mothma, former Senator of Chandrila. She had been the subject of close monitoring by the ISB due to her rather public critic-ism of the Empire's expanding military policies. In an act of treason on the senate floor, she gave voice and legitimacy to the Emperor's enemies in the public record. It came as no surprise to the ISB that she would ultimately betray the Emperor, and publicly declare herself as part of the growing rebellion. In

a moment that shocked the galaxy, she identified the Emperor by name as the galaxy's greatest menace, and made a public declaration of rebellion, creating a period of civil war. Immediately after this action, the Emperor demanded the ISB compile a full dossier on her political allies and compatriots for targeted reprisal. Mothma's most frequent ally, Senator Bail Organa, was by then only a part-time delegate in the senate, and had a spotless record of support in comparison to Mothma's rhetoric. But

nonetheless, such affiliation put the Royal House of Alderaan on the scanners of ISB. Bail Organa and his daughter, Senator Leia Organa, were closely monitored. Evidence of Alderaan's open support for the Rebel Alliance led to swift and decisive action carried out by Grand Moff Wilhuff Tarkin.

Whatever personal notes Andressa Divo had compiled regarding Bail Organa vanished that day, according to her journal logs. It also marked the last time she spoke with her father.

ARRESTING OFFICER // DAINE JIR (ON BEHALF OF GOVERNOR WILHUFF TARKIN)

WARRANT

ANNOTATION: SCHEDULE FOR IMMEDIATE TERMINATION

LEIA ORGANA

HEIGHT: 1.5M

GENDER: FEMALE

SPECIES: HUMAN

HOMEWORLD: ALDERAAN

FILE / 7977.331.3

WARRANT: LEIA ORGANA

Diplomatic immunity could only extend so far. It came as a surprise to some in the upper echelons of the Empire that Lord Vader issued an arrest-on-sight decree for Leia Organa after spotting her personal consular ship, the *Tantive IV*, departing a restricted Imperial zone and site of a major rebel incursion at the Battle of Scarif. Officer Daine Jir recorded in his report that Princess Organa claimed diplomatic immunity and ambassadorial privilege, denying any knowledge of rebel activity.

It was a tactic known to be used by sympathetic senators, hiding behind diplomatic shields to avoid the scrutiny of the law. That the Royal House of Alderaan's humanitarian gestures engendered public support, goodwill, and popularity in the senate proved making accusations against them a political minefield, unless the Empire had ironclad evidence of wrongdoing. The desperate bid to escape Scarif proved to be Organa's undoing. Though Vader and his officers spread word of her arrest among specific channels, news of her capture was kept out of the media. Instead, the Empire announced that the *Tantive IV* was destroyed in a catastrophic meteor collision, killing all on board.

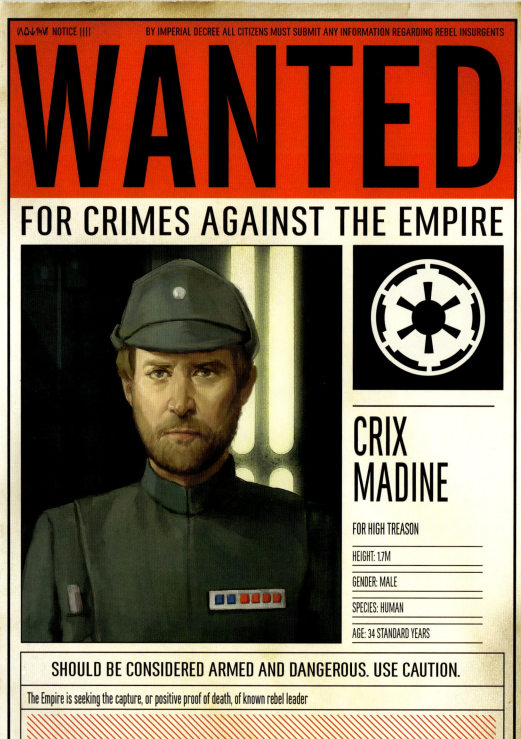

ꓥꓷꓦꓥꓦ NOTICE ꓲꓲꓲꓲ — BY IMPERIAL DECREE ALL CITIZENS MUST SUBMIT ANY INFORMATION REGARDING REBEL INSURGENTS

WANTED

FOR CRIMES AGAINST THE EMPIRE

CRIX MADINE

FOR HIGH TREASON

HEIGHT: 1.7M

GENDER: MALE

SPECIES: HUMAN

AGE: 34 STANDARD YEARS

SHOULD BE CONSIDERED ARMED AND DANGEROUS. USE CAUTION.

The Empire is seeking the capture, or positive proof of death, of known rebel leader

It is the will of Emperor Palpatine to ensure the future of a stable and prosperous galaxy

FILE / 7977.535.1

WANTED: CRIX MADINE

Once the leader of a crack Imperial commando unit, Crix Madine defected from service to join the growing rebellion, a move that stunned the upper echelons of the Imperial military. An Imperial "cleaner team" known as Inferno Squad quickly locked down all information that Madine had been given access to in order to get an understanding of the possible Imperial secrets that would now be in the hands of the Rebellion. Agent Divo assisted in the damage control that followed Madine's treachery. From her notes:

This is what the ISB is supposed to root out, and I consider it a personal failure that I did not predict the defection of Crix Madine. That such a skilled commando could harbor doubts to the Imperial cause is a blow to morale among the ISB and the military. He has made a personal enemy of any Imperial who believed in him or sacrificed so much to the greater cause of the New Order.

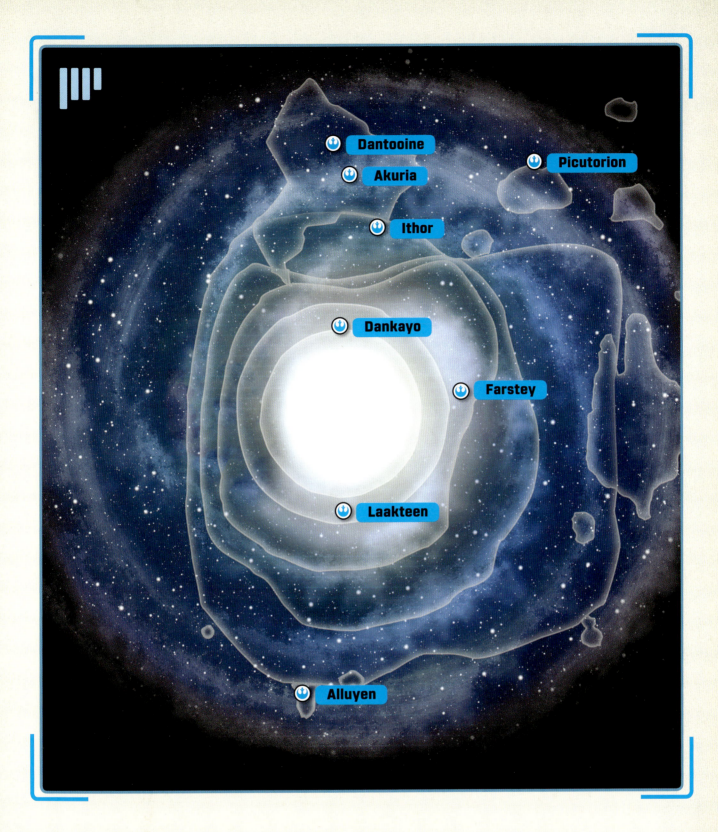

Dantooine

Akuria

Picutorion

Ithor

Dankayo

Farstey

Laakteen

Alluyen

FILE / 7980.011.1

SUSPECTED REBEL BASE LOCATIONS

Law enforcement intelligence reports were routinely chopped, sifted, and reconstituted by Imperial Intelligence and the Imperial Security Bureau in attempts to find possible locations for Rebel Alliance outposts. Because of reprisals on populated worlds such as Garel and Ghorman, in which civilians took extensive collateral damage during raids, the rebels took to avoiding inhabited worlds, and instead favored unsettled planets. The rebels also often exploited old smuggler routes to avoid law enforcement patrols. On a quarterly basis, the military intelligence agencies demanded a collated review of suspicious activity reports and reverse-mapped it to population studies, zeroing in on cases that clustered on sparsely settled areas of the galaxy. These were then probability-studied by AI predictors to generate a prioritized target list for the Imperial probe droid surveys that scoured the spacelanes in the years following the Battle of Yavin.

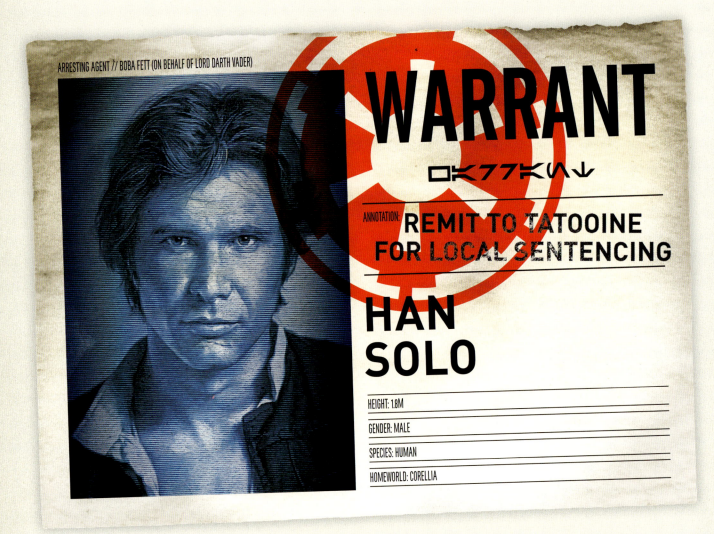

ARRESTING AGENT // BOBA FETT (ON BEHALF OF LORD DARTH VADER)

WARRANT

ꝏꝏꝏꝏꝏꝏꝏ

ANNOTATION: **REMIT TO TATOOINE FOR LOCAL SENTENCING**

HAN SOLO

HEIGHT: 1.8M

GENDER: MALE

SPECIES: HUMAN

HOMEWORLD: CORELLIA

FILE / 7956.919.5

WARRANT: HAN SOLO

Culled from data collectors inside the carbon-freezing chambers of Cloud City on Bespin, these holographic reconstructions depict the fate that may have befallen an enemy of Jabba the Hutt. Encased in a block of industrial carbonite was the form of Han Solo, Corellian smuggler and associate of the rebel group responsible for the destruction of the Death Star. Solo had numerous bounties on his head, for his past crimes and for his role in the rebellion. With his Imperial imprisonment denied, this data record became the sole evidence of his capture. As Agent Divo wrote:

Han Solo was one of the ones that got away. Once the identity of the Millennium Falcon was confirmed as the YT-1300 freighter that participated in the Battle of Yavin, Solo joined the ranks of the Empire's most wanted—a position he already held within criminal circles. It would turn out to be a race between bounty hunters working for the Hutt criminal syndicates and the Empire for Solo's capture. It is with frustration that I learned that Lord Vader handed over Solo to a bounty hunter for delivery back to Jabba the Hutt rather than let him return to Imperial custody. However, I am in no position to question Lord Vader's decisions on this matter.

98

SCUM AND VILLAINY

A FATE SEALED IN CARBONITE

The peculiar stasis qualities of carbonite have been known in the galaxy for centuries, as ancient sleeper ships that expanded the pre-Republic borders relied upon extended hibernation to keep the crew alive as they traveled across unfathomable distances. The use of carbonite for organic hibernation faded away as hyperdrives did away with the need for such lengthy voyages, and bio-entropic field generators became the norm in medical applications. Carbon freezing thus became the standard for industrial applications, such as the freezing of coaxium, tibanna, and other volatile substances for transport. With some modifications, however, these carbon-freezing chambers could be equipped to entrap living cargo, subjecting them to a painful stasis that has been described as "a big wide-awake nothing." Imperials, bounty hunters, and some gangsters have been known to use carbonite in this crude but effective way. The earliest known trophies of this variety date back to the ancient Krath that conquered the carbonite mines of the Empress Teta system, thousands of years ago in the galaxy's dark past.

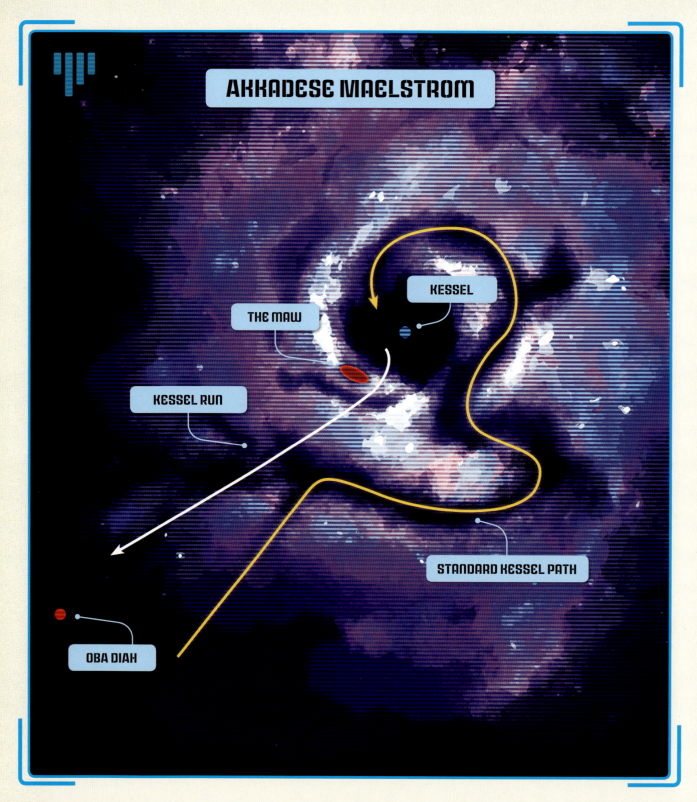

AKKADESE MAELSTROM

KESSEL

THE MAW

KESSEL RUN

STANDARD KESSEL PATH

OBA DIAH

SCUM AND VILLAINY

FILE / 7969.111.1

KESSEL RUN MAP

The planet Kessel rests within an occluded area of space known as the Akkadese Maelstrom. A slowly swirling tangle of clear channels wind their way through the ionized gas and dust clouds, with the most reliable routes marked by positional space buoys. Beyond the channels are dense banks of gas that conceal enormous carbonbergs, static discharges, concentrated water vapor and ammonia weather cells, and gravity wells. Only the most daring pilots with the fastest hyperdrives and sophisticated navicomputers dare wander off the marked paths for jumps shorter than the methodically plotted Kessel Run that measures more than 20 parsecs in length. The most foolhardy or insane risk passage through Gedder's Pass, Black Rock Passage, or near the space-bending singularity known as the Maw in an attempt to shave time and meandering distance off their run.

Agent Divo wrote:

So meaningless is the life of a smuggler that they would risk all well-being for an illegal record of distinction only known in the underworld. Have they nothing of more worth to live for? Evidently not, if this is the kind of livelihood they are drawn to.

ANDRESSA DIVO

FILE / 7975.242.2

SEIZED CONTRABAND

Seventeen crates of spice contraband were found aboard a scuttled *Gozanti* cruiser floating off the Perlemian trade route. It was most likely a smuggling vessel that escaped from a pirate ambush only to succumb to extensive damage. A careful analysis of the cargo revealed Kessel spice mixed with a number of potentially dangerous impurities to help extend its limited supply.

From Agent Divo's notes:

There is nothing in this galaxy quite as porous as the cargo security around Kessel, since it proves so profitable to look the other way as spice shipments "fall off" the legitimate medical manifests. This is a chronic problem that no one seems too interested in solving as long as the credits flow.

These crates contained 400 kilograms of "Kessel spice," which turned out to be only thirty percent pure. *It was laced with powdered bacta derivative, nysillin, synthetized glycerine, and some sort of wood pulp. The markings on the pressure crates point to a small smuggling ring out of the Lothal sector. I've passed along a report to Governor Pryce, but she has shown little interest in following up.*

II

THE CHALLENGES OF THE NEW REPUBLIC

The transition from Empire to Republic was a chaotic torrent of change compared to the slow-boil transformation of the Republic to the Empire. After decades of Imperial rule, the weary galaxy was receptive to something different. Reaching a consensus on what ways things would be different proved to be the real challenge. The fragile provisional government needed to focus its efforts in organizing the chaos of an otherwise directionless galaxy. While law and order was a priority, it was understandably just a single point in an endless list of things to be fixed.

The fledgling New Republic judiciary had its hands full decoding and navigating the mazelike Imperial Office of Criminal Investigation's datacore. To its dismay, it found political enemies ranked alongside thieves, assailants, and murderers. Overstated charges were hard to separate from legitimate arrest warrants. Some in the New Republic entertained the notion of simply granting fresh-start clemency, but thankfully cooler heads prevailed.

As this probe into the state of the criminal justice system took place, the New Republic began to take shape. It became clear that the authoritarian overreach of the Empire would not in any way be tolerated. The New Republic favored decentralization, with more and more responsibility being shouldered by member worlds. This new galactic government would be less imposing, and individual systems could adopt a more customized approach to law enforcement. Idealists who championed individualism and self-determination rejoiced.

Realists, who knew the inherent disarray of such an approach, steeled themselves for the hard work ahead.

Crime is the most resilient of parasites. It found a way to thrive under the jackbooted heels of the Empire. In today's more relaxed climate, it was allowed to spread. Criminals pursued by local authorities could disappear into a more lenient system with a simple hyperspace jump. Whole sector governments became subject to corruption. Mobsters became oligarchs, absorbing abandoned pieces of Imperial infrastructure with surprising ease.

The New Republic Senate tried to emphasize the freedoms that had returned to the public. But opponents to the new system were right to call out its shortcomings. The pendulum has swung too far, they said. It took years to find an equilibrium, which came in the form of the Sector Rangers—coordinated law enforcement that spanned borders and shared information. But by the time the Rangers were instituted, new criminal organizations, which evolved from the Hutt cartels, the Crymorah syndicate and Crimson Dawn, had become powerful. The New Republic was but a fraction of the size of the Galactic Empire and even the Old Republic that preceded it. Its blunted authority can only reach so far.

Are critics of the New Republic right? Is it too soft on crime? The case files and examples that follow are proof of the insidious crime that faces our new government and the strength of the criminal organizations that have taken hold in the galaxy. They are also, I hope, proof of the hard work we put in to ensuring the safety of our citizens.

FILE / 7996.441.3

GRADUATION OF EXANTOR DIVO

My mother attended my graduation at the Hosnian Prime Academy of Law Enforcement, Class of '96 (Hosnian Reckoning), though I did not know it at the time. Ours was not the only family strained by the shifting tides of history, by the changes that turned galactic governance inside out. My mother was loyal to the Empire. She had assumed the New Republic would execute her as an enemy of their state. It took much convincing to have her emerge from a life on the run, a life I was blessedly too young to comprehend or remember.

The Republic eventually impressed upon her that she did not warrant arrest or punishment given her record, which was meticulously researched by the new chiefs of law enforcement. She was instead offered an invitation to help the fledgling government with her expertise. She pointedly refused. She was a proud woman not willing to acknowledge a government she deemed illegitimate. She kept that fire of resentment burning for years.

My enrollment in the Academy, with the aim of being a Sector Ranger, did not sit well with her but she did not try to stop me. I focused on my studies, kept the politics out of my correspondence with her, and accepted that this would forever be a wedge between us.

I later found this holo among my mother's things, an image of that proud day captured with a long lens. I did not recognize it as one of the standard set provided by the school. She revealed that she had taken it. She had never told me that she had attended, for she did not want to distract me. It was then, she told me, that we, as people with the tradition of law enforcement in our veins, do not often get the luxury of choosing the laws we enforce. She admitted to having misgivings, particularly in the latter years of the Empire, with Imperial policy, but she had no outlet to talk about it.

She did not want me to face that same isolation. She made me a promise that if I ever had doubts about the New Republic and its direction, I would have someone to talk to.

FILE / 8009.332.1

NEW REPUBLIC PATROL

A trio of New Republic patrollers on duty strolls through a crowded shopping thoroughfare in Hanna City, Chandrila, in what could pass for a posed public relations image. It is in fact captured candidly from security holocams placed strategically around the plaza. This was the peaceful melding of cultures that, if you were to believe the New Republic senate, would have been impossible to find during the time of the Empire.

Such hyperbole does little favor to the intended point: that such peace is more widespread than it was in the past. But the New Republic holds no exclusivity on such tranquility, nor over the effective use of law enforcement. Many Imperial policies still hold true when it comes to policing, which were in fact holdovers from the days of the Old Republic. It's not the police officer's job to comment on politics. Nor is it the officer's job, strictly speaking, to be used as a prop in political posturing. But such is a side effect of being a cop, and has been since the first clan leader erected a watch on ancient town borders.

106

FILE / 7981.345.1

VORAS THE HUTT HOLO IMAGE

One of the subjects of study in the academy, and indeed the focus of a research essay I wrote as part of an entrance exam into the Sector Rangers, was Voras the Hutt. The peculiar circumstances of the Anoat sector have provided scholars with a fascinating model of how the fallout of the Empire's demise might have turned out differently galaxy-wide.

When word of the Emperor's death spread from Endor to the Anoat sector, there was cause for celebration, as it heralded the dawn of a free age. It wasn't

an evacuation, however, but rather a redistribution of Imperial assets by Governor Ubrik Adelhard within the sector. He took steps to lock the region down. He propagated a tale that the Alliance victory at Endor was a lie, but still the Empire was besieged by terrorism, and for security's sake, he needed to lock down his local sector.

Within those borders, inside the so-called Iron Blockade, Voras the Hutt was a deeply ensconced crime lord, head of the nebulous Ivax Syndicate. The forced

isolation of the sector shook up the balance of criminal operations, as shortages spiked the value of the black market. With the Ivax profits cannibalized by rivals, the normally apolitical Voras emerged from the shadows and took a more active role in assisting the local uprising who challenged the Imperials.

This sociopolitical microcosm has been examined by scholars and has been the subject of computer models in universities and academies as a study of dynamics within closed systems.

FILE / 7981.345.1

DEEP SURVEILLANCE OF WIND TUNNEL

After the fall of the Iron Blockade, Cloud City once again underwent liberation, and Baron Administrator Lando Calrissian reclaimed his title abandoned during the Imperial occupation. Calrissian and his police administrators spent much time sorting through holographic recordings of the occupation and the uprising that toppled it in an effort to understand the historic events. Among the images uncovered was evidence of a method

the Ivax Syndicate used to dispose of its enemies.

As pictured here, Nogba Quush, Ivax enforcer, is inside Cloud City's vast central wind tunnel, dealing with a treacherous henchbeing who had been selling Ivax secrets to a rival cartel. After shaking out information from the victim (which defied capture by audio sensors in the wind-filled tunnel), Quush let the subject plummet into the depths. Reclamation vents

funneled the victim to the outer surface of the city, after capturing any loose metal or plastic components and shunting them to the reclamation furnaces.

The Ivax Syndicate scattered after Cloud City's liberation, freed from the blockade that kept it cloistered in the Anoat sector. Calrissian declined to continue any pursuit, reasoning that he'd deal with them should they ever surface in his jurisdiction again.

FILE / 8011.110.3

MEGALOX BETA INCURSION SECURITY FOOTAGE

Megalox is a high-security prison kept isolated by the heavy gravity that exists on the planet Megalox Beta. A repulsor field creates an area of standard gravity within the prison, but escape from the prison is made impossible by the crushing conditions beyond. Security recordings of an attempted breakout, masterminded by notorious prisoner Grakkus the Hutt, captured images of humanoid accomplices in unmarked black combat fatigues.

A close-up examination of these recordings confirm that one of the intruders is Poe Dameron, former New Republic pilot and known associate of the Resistance movement. It is exactly these kinds of extralegal activities that raise the ire of law enforcement and make General Leia Organa's movement so toxic in New Republic politics.

When questioned on the matter, General Organa insisted her agents were merely there to question Grakkus, and that the Hutt and First Order agents took advantage of their presence to sow chaos. But her excuses once again rely on mercurial evidence and the presence of a First Order conspiracy that is simply not supported by the facts.

ZOOM

400X

FILE / 8004.401.3

AMAXINE WARRIORS HOLO IMAGE

The fragmentation of galactic government has led to dangerous information gaps that greatly complicate the maintenance of security. Independent sector states guard their domestic secrets from their neighbors. This cloistering allowed the rise of the Amaxine Warriors, an apparent militia power that now controls smuggling operations in a patch of the Outer Rim Territories. There is virtually no information about the makeup of this group, or their origins.

Their name appeals to aficionados of deep galactic history—the legendary Amaxines from centuries ago, in the age of the Old Republic. These ancient warriors vanished in time, but whoever these current chaos agents are, they brandish their standard as if they were legitimate heirs. At first, New Republic Intelligence assumed reports of these warriors were describing mercenary armies, available for hire by worlds that could not raise their own military.

But as those reports were expanded, the accounts of piracy and smuggling threw those initial thoughts into doubt.

As of now, the New Republic only has scattered and piecemeal accounts of their activities. The secretive Amaxines have proven to be apolitical, with no demands or statements illustrating their point of view. I do believe them to be mercenaries—proxy agents—but the question remains, who pays them?

WANTED

CONSIDERED DANGEROUS

NAME: RINNRIVIN DI

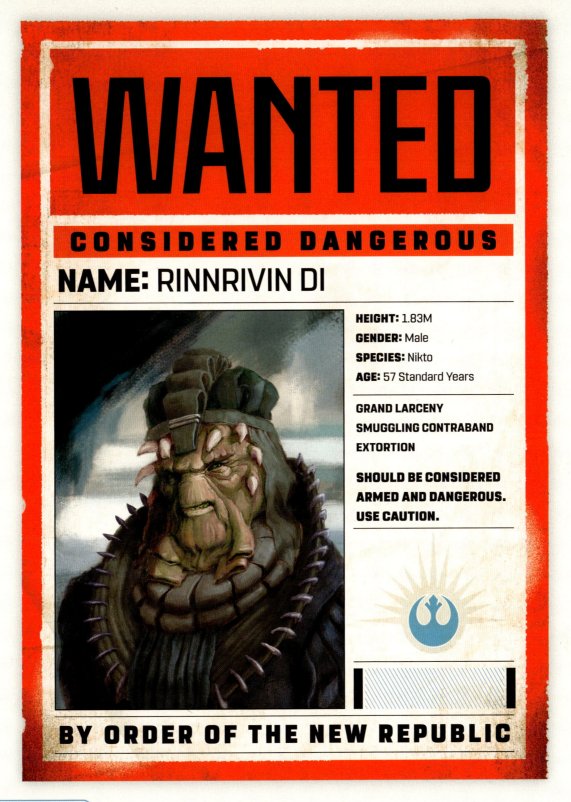

HEIGHT: 1.83M
GENDER: Male
SPECIES: Nikto
AGE: 57 Standard Years

GRAND LARCENY
SMUGGLING CONTRABAND
EXTORTION

SHOULD BE CONSIDERED
ARMED AND DANGEROUS.
USE CAUTION.

BY ORDER OF THE NEW REPUBLIC

FILE / 8004.321.2

WANTED: RINNRIVIN DI

Crime in the Outer Rim underwent a transformation independent of the socio-political one of the Empire to Republic, because the death of Jabba the Hutt came so close to the Battle of Endor. Those within the Hutt crime families anxiously awaited a successor to emerge, but infighting and intrigue led to a waning of power. Stepping into this vacuum was Rinnrivin Di, a Nikto smuggler and cartel operative with uncanny business acumen.

Di keeps his operations beyond the New Republic borders, making it difficult to monitor. His ample cash flow is hard to track as it is shuffled through front companies situated well outside our borders. Our allies on Ryloth have expressed concern to the New Republic Senate that his shipping vessels are encroaching upon their space.

Where the Hutts inspired fear, Rinnrivin Di has charisma in droves, and he uses it to his advantage. Di subverts the unfortunate stereotypes that have painted the Nikto culture as unsophisticated brutes. His clothing and tastes in art and cuisine would be at home in the Core, and are often disarming. By forcing some to question their assumptions about Nikto culture, he hides what their instincts are telling them: that he is a criminal, through and through.

FILE / 8004.121.4

SIDON ITHANO AND CREW HOLO IMAGES

The gentleman pirate is an oxymoronic concept that the media and popular culture cannot help but fixate upon. Romanticizing lawlessness—the perceived freedom that comes with breaking the rules—is as old as storytelling. Would it surprise some to know that a pirate such as Sidon Ithano runs a business, with a ledger, dependents, and investments? The maxim "crime doesn't pay" may be an outdated and naïve idea, but the idea

that "crime is hard work" might help dispel more fanciful notions and keep people from daydreaming about the life of an interstellar brigand.

Sidon Ithano spends a great deal of time and effort honing his brand. He has cultivated an aura of adventurism, from his devilish demeanor, to the sweep of his Kaleesh helmet and his colorful aliases as the Red Raider, the Crimson Corsair, or the Blood Buccaneer. Flying aboard

his ship *Meson Martinet*, Ithano has been known to leave red sigils in the shape of his helmet delivered via dye detonators on the hulls of captured ships. Aside from First Mate Quiggod, Ithano's crew—a rotating roster that currently includes a Rutian Twi'lek named Reveth, an Ishi Tib named Pendewqell, an unknown Onadone, a Gamorrean named Squeaky—are all trained to, whenever possible, enhance their captain's reputation.

FILE / 8011.001.1

GRUMMGAR HOLO IMAGE

In law enforcement's ongoing quest to win the public's confidence, we've found some success in showing the effects of crime not on vulnerable sentients, but rather on the subsentient animal life. Though I don't agree with this, I can see where such a case can be made. Sentients targeting sentients is part of our particular survival chain, and some have grown callous, disregarding such repeated crimes. But when crimes target the animal kingdom, exploiting or harming creatures simply trying to survive, it has the potential to cut through to the disaffected and be more disturbing.

This is Grummgar, a big game hunter and poacher active in the independent Outer Rim and Western Reaches. This hulking Dowutin landed on the New Republic crime scanner when Ithorian representatives reported a heretical violation of their sacred Mother Jungle, the vast rain forest ecosystem that covers their homeworld. A holo shows an unknown Ithorian accomplice, undoubtedly compensated by Grummgar, standing with the poacher over the body of a molsume. The Ithorians rightly focused on the desecration of one of their most holy laws—setting foot within the Mother Jungle—by one of their own. But the rest of the New Republic, when shown this image, focused on the fact that Grummgar posted it himself to the HoloNet, in an act of brazen defiance.

FILE / 8011.001.0

ILLEGAL HUNTING ENCODED ADVERT

Following up on the investigation of Grummgar's HoloNet activity, a decryption of deeply encoded data tucked in the margins of the public access infocache revealed smuggled messages offering big game hunting expeditions of an illegal nature. A different Ithorian hunter appears in this image than the one that accompanied Grummgar, suggesting perhaps the existence of an Ithorian organization that is exploiting its most sacred grounds.

An examination of deeper linked data, beyond the surface text, revealed a list of game available for capture, which included fauna native to Ithor as well as transplanted wildlife presumably let loose in the Mother Jungle for hunting. It would appear that the Ithorians' reverence for the jungle—which has resulted in the Ithorians keeping their distance from it—has left it vulnerable to such exploitation.

FILE / 8011.001.1

KANJIKLUB RAID AFTERMATH HOLO

The decline of the Hutts as criminal overlords freed client species, indentured cultures, and other former underlings from their stifling rule. Most notable of these groups is Kanjiklub, made up of pit fighters from the enslaved human colonists on the Hutt world of Nar Kanji. An uprising in the pits sent the Hutts and their bodyguards fleeing, letting the newly liberated humans retake their colony. Rather than find peace, this society is now held in thrall by Kanjiklub, who rules Nar Kanji protectively in determination to never again let any intruders on their world.

As Kanjiklub has attempted to spread its territory, it has come into contact with the New Republic. An attempted incursion in the outer Kegan system was thwarted by local New Republic police forces after a forty-six-hour standoff and gunfight managed to capture four Kanjiklubbers at the cost of twenty-five police officers' lives.

FILE / 8011.001.2

CAPTURED KANJI WEAPONS

Kanjiklub weaponry is often crude and brutish; any sophisticated features and decorative filigree are scraped off in favor of basic functionality. The most seasoned of pit fighters from the enslaved days often decorate their weapons with personal totems, such as bones from gladiators or creatures they bested. From the Kegan uprising, we are afforded a closer look at some of their deadliest tools.

Kanjiklubbers are not the only criminals to use cage-boosted blaster rifles, but they have made a mark using them. An accelerator cage encloses the blaster barrel and the galven-circuitry within that collimates the energy into an explosive blaster bolt. The cage boosts the destructive potential of each bolt beyond the safety limits dictated by the standard barrel. This also makes the blasters searing hot to the touch.

Due to their shorter barrel lengths, similar caging effects cannot be used on blaster pistols, but the Kanjiklubbers have found ways to enhance their deadliness. The stripping of static damper prongs within the blaster make for hazier blaster bolts that increase in size, regardless of the bore of the barrel, but at the risks of explosive misfires or weapon burnout.

Because a Kanjiklub blaster will short out due to these abusive modifications, they are often equipped with vibro-bayonets, bone clubs, stun cords, or other painful contact surfaces that turn the otherwise useless firearm into a melee weapon.

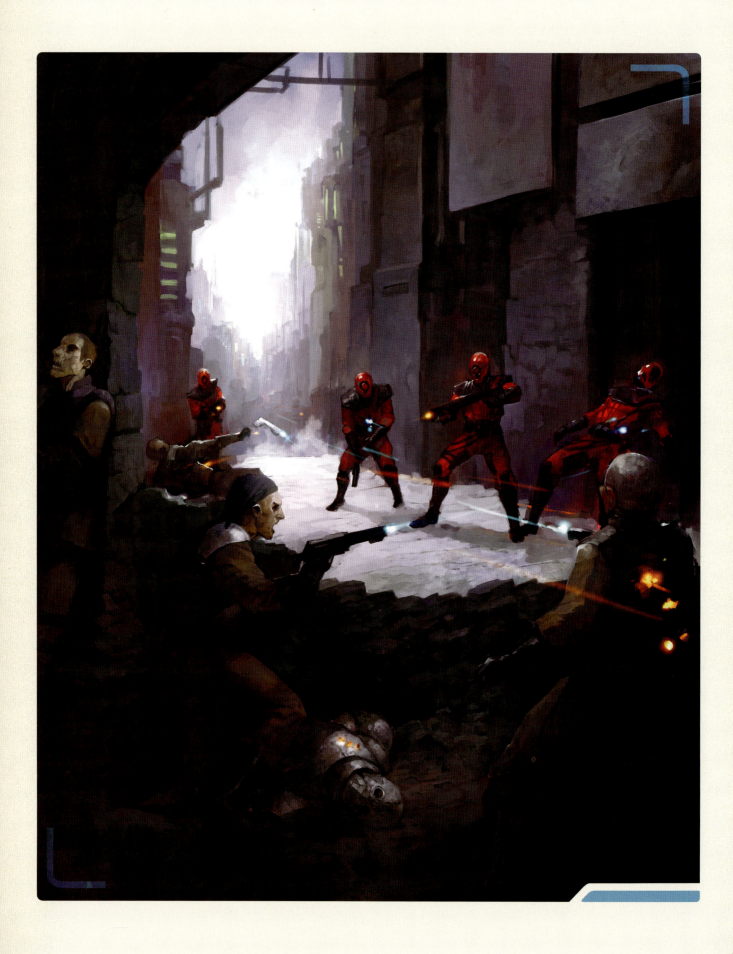

GUAVIAN DEATH GANG HOLO AND SOLDIERS

Another up-and-coming criminal organization in the current era is the Guavian Death Gang. Research into what scant evidence exists indicates they originated from high-tech mercenaries, formerly based out of the Core Worlds. As the Core settled into order under the New Republic, the Guavian ancestors relocated to the more lawless sectors of the Outer Rim, bringing with them a technological advantage from the inner worlds.

Holographic imagery recorded by private security forces on Croluthe Zenj shows the Guavian Death Gang in action. Their remarkable silent coordination over distances suggests a well-shielded communication network keeping them in constant contact with one another. This, and their advanced weaponry, gave them a sizable advantage in this engagement.

An examination of captured Guavian soldiers revealed not only taciturn, well-trained individuals that resisted interrogation, but examples of high-end cybernetic surgical work. These soldiers were modified beyond organic standards, with bolstered circulatory and sensory systems. Laws governing surgical modification are the responsibility of individual sectors and have become impossible to enforce on a galactic level. Some speculate that the Guavian surgical work has the markers of Dr. Cornelius Evazan, or a protégé.

120

FILE / 8011.711.3

BACKGROUND: KING PRANA

King Grevoth Prana IX is the monarch of the Kaboryth cluster, a dozen star systems gifted to a royal family by the Old Republic. Today, the cluster continues as a quaint throwback to olden days. Its principal contribution to the New Republic is as a source of foodstuffs. The cultivated fields across the pasture moons in the twelve systems are a bountiful trove. This gives Prana and his worlds political pull in the Core Worlds, allowing him to operate with relative impunity, where some of the more questionable aspects of his regency are chalked up to "cultural exceptions" by a New Republic that does not want to meddle.

For example, Prana is involved in a sizable trade of exotic creatures that would ordinarily be deemed illegal. Prana maintains a menagerie that rivals the Coruscant Zoo of old, but, provided his acquisitions meet the standards of culturally enriching acquisitions, they need not adhere to otherwise standard laws. In practice, though, unscrupulous traders attempt to give Prana "gifts," illegally obtained and transported creatures, for addition to his collection.

FILE / 8011.801.4

EVIDENCE: CARGO FOR PRANA

A captured cargo vessel destined for Regent Solculvis of Mol'leaj revealed an alarming assortment of exotic creatures prohibited by law for private ownership. The ship, *Sketter's Quarrel*, was found dead in space. Its crew had been stung to death by kheilwar wasps escaped from a damaged shipping container. Among the exotics cataloged by the Sector Rangers were a Tralusian styanax, a sycanid from Humbarine, an Arkanian polar drake, Outer Rim worrts, and a dwarf rathtar from Trillia.

Regent Solculvis controls territory that neighbors that of King Prana, and the two have had a longstanding rivalry when it comes to the collection of exotics. As Solculvis does not currently enjoy a favored status within the New Republic— his regency is independent—cargoes captured en route to his worlds are subject to the transit laws of their origin port.

122

FILE / 8010.364.3

CANTO CRIME SCENE

The planet Cantonica is in the Corporate Sector, the storied fiefdom erected during the Republic era as an in-de-pendent state, free of regulations. Cantonica evolved to become the playground for the rich, a resort world with luxurious entertainment centered on the port city of Canto Bight. The planet exists beyond the reach of the New Republic, but a strategic agree-ment between our governments has allowed an exchange of information between law enforcement agencies on both sides of the sector border. Though rife with financial crime, the Corporate Sector does not want more violent crime to spill into their burnished centers.

The Canto Bight Police Department (CBPD) has been in quarterly communication per standard year with our offices. Commissioner Heethra Fansoff leads the exchange of information, which includes summaries of exceptional police work, unsolved cases, and lists of suspects and allies. Pictured in this representative file, Officer Randus Codille stands over a disabled valet droid found to possess an extrascopic sensory apparatus that would allegedly give a suspect an edge in gambling.

123

FILE / 8010.364.2

CANTO BIGHT SURVEILLANCE

The Canto Casino and Hotel complex is deeply entrenched in local politics as it not only plays host to noteworthy councilors and legislators from offworld as well as on, but it also is a major source of income to the beachside city. Ordinarily, its administrators would balk at sharing surveillance footage of any kind, as it is a privately owned facility and dedicated to protecting the privacy of its clientele.

However, an exchange of information between the New Republic and Canto law enforcement was agreed to at a higher level than the hotel leadership staff.

After some negotiation, the heads of security agreed to share the imagery but only after having reviewed it themselves, to allow the deletion or obscuring of certain clientele who paid extra for discretion.

124

FILE / 8010.321.2

STURG GANNA SURVEILLANCE

Councilor Sturg Ganna—a onetime lawyer, holo-show host, and boisterous politician—has served as part of the Canto Bight legislative body for over twenty years. He holds the dubious distinction of being forced to resign from office due to felony convictions, but was reelected to office after returning from prison. A hulking Whippomorn, Sturg Ganna is bet-

ter known among the residents of Canto Bight as "Big Sturg" and is beloved by a broad cross-section of his constituents. His past convictions include assault and embezzlement, but the smooth-talking Ganna emphasizes the crimes as part of his impetuous charm.

Sturg Ganna is seemingly untouchable by CBPD and the Corporate Sector

Authority police due to his appeal and the fact that his business acumen adds to the city's coffers. Though he is beyond the jurisdiction of the New Republic, just knowing who Sturn does business with has been of help to our law enforcement officers. Sturg undoubtedly knows he's being watched by us and flaunts the attention.

FILE / 8010.322.1

SURVEILLANCE OF ANGLANG LEHET

Another being of interest known to haunt the casinos of Canto Bight is Anglang Lehet, an enforcer for the Cularin Syndicate. The syndicate set up a satellite operation on Canto Bight, awarding Lehet a station on the resort world as a reward for his loyal service over the decades. This was when Canto Bight was but a fraction of its current size. As casinos grew in size and opulence, the syndicate, who preferred smaller, seedier casinos for their business dealings, departed the resort world. Lehet stayed, essentially retiring on the resort world. It is unknown if he is still a syndicate operative or not, but the CBPD keeps an eye on him and has not turned up anything overly incriminating aside from contact with a small outfit called the Old City Boys. Over a century old, Lehet has become a mentor of sorts to up-and-coming criminals, who seek out his guidance in exchange for a tutoring fee. CBPD allows Lehet to carry out this business untouched as they can then identify his students and share their profiles between the CBPD and the New Republic. Lehet is aware of this surveillance and considers it part of an education. If a would-be grifter, hit man, thief, or other criminal can escape notice, then he or she will be stronger for it.

AFTERWORD

The generations of law enforcement service in my family has, admittedly, skewed my perception. It has made it easy to think of police duty as an island, detached from the tides that shape the galaxy—the washing out of the Republic, the crushing wave of the Empire, and the bringing in of the New Republic.

The focus of law enforcement is to serve the people by fighting the crimes that threaten their safety. This was, to my thinking, separate from the government. The hindsight gained from touring these case files, and seeing the attitudes exhibited by my grandfather and mother, is illuminating. While I may chastise those who have a naïve view of law enforcement, I myself have had a naïve view of its relation to galactic government. It is,

in humbling review, far too easy for the long arm of the law to be manipulated by interests other than the public good. So too is it naïve to think that the crimes within a local jurisdiction are isolated incidents. The source or root cause may lie on the other side of the galaxy. The shifting power struggles within the galaxy shape crime and criminal organizations similar to how they manipulate attitudes among the people and law enforcement.

In addition to the vigilance every officer must cultivate against crime, we must be wary of agendas coming from the capital, be it Coruscant, Chandrila, Hosnian Prime, or a local government. Sprees or trends in the types of crimes and criminals one faces can be an indication

of a greater threat. To that end, I leave you with an excerpt from the New Republic's law enforcement charter. Words I read for clarity and purpose, words that are bundled in the oath I took to serve the New Republic and its people.

". . . our primary function shall be the maintenance of lawful order through the elimination of all agents, foreign and domestic, seeking to undermine the lawful authority of the New Republic . . . as the maintenance of peace can only be ensured when the rights of all sentient beings, regardless of species, origin, or philosophy, are respected, our agents shall dedicate themselves to safeguarding those rights, and to bring to justice any and all violator, wherever they may be found."

ACKNOWLEDGEMENTS

After *Star Wars Propaganda* had wrapped, I appreciated what a unique and fun project that was—a tome written from the perspective of a specific author who lived in the *Star Wars* universe. It was an exception to my usual approach to writing guides, which aimed to have the author be as invisible and unbiased as possible. When the opportunity arose to follow *Propaganda* up with something new but similar, I jumped at the chance.

I want to thank my editor Delia Greve, for once again extending an invitation to write a *Star Wars* book with an intriguing point of view. And in Lucasfilm's publishing group, I thank Frank Parisi for getting this ball rolling, and Samantha Holland for guiding it through its formative stages and to its end. As always thanks to Michael Siglain for letting me contribute to the *Star Wars* library, and those in the Lucasfilm Story Group—mainly Kiri Hart and James Waugh—for encouraging my work as an author.

This book wouldn't exist if not for the talented artists who have brought its words and ideas to life with these wonderful illustrations. Special thanks to these artists, and to senior graphic designer, Sam Dawson, for coordinating their work and shaping the look of this book.

Like all things *Star Wars*, this builds on what has come before, and is indebted to George Lucas for giving us such a rich setting to explore. More specifically, I want to thank authors Michael Allen Horne and Rick D. Stuart, who wrote some deeply entertaining guidebooks during the drought years *Star Wars*, when the old roleplaying game was one of the few sources of new content. Their dedication to meticulous world-building is evident in their guides that touched on the subject of crime and law enforcement and was influential to this work.

Brimming with creative inspiration, how-to projects, and useful information to enrich your everyday life, Quarto Knows is a favorite destination for those pursuing their interests and passions. Visit our site and dig deeper with our books into your area of interest: Quarto Creates, Quarto Cooks, Quarto Homes, Quarto Lives, Quarto Drives, Quarto Explores, Quarto Gifts, or Quarto Kids.

Disney · LUCASFILM

© & TM 2018 Lucasfilm.
www.starwars.com

For Lucasfilm:
Editor: Samantha Holland
Creative Director of Publishing: Michael Siglain
Art Director: Troy Alders
Story Group: Leland Chee and Matt Martin

Published in 2018 by Epic Ink, an imprint of The Quarto Group, 11120 NE 33rd Place, Suite 201, Bellevue, WA 98004 USA.
www.QuartoKnows.com

18 19 20 21 22   5 4 3 2 1

ISBN: 978-0-7603-6205-1

Library of Congress Cataloging-in-Publication Data available upon request.

Author: Pablo Hidalgo
Illustration: Raph Lomotan: pages 9, 13, 14, 22, 27, 28, 29, 32-33, 36, 44, 46, 53, 92, 99, 101, 103, 126; Ronan Le Fur: pages 2, 10-11, 54-55, 104-105; Russell Walks: pages 5, 37, 45 (left), 50, 65, 71, 73, 75, 82-83; Will Biks: 23, 45 (right), 47 (bottom); Gunship Revolution: pages 12, 15, 21, 24, 25, 26, 35, 38, 41, 42-43, 48-49, 51, 66, 67, 68, 70, 72, 74, 76, 78, 80, 81, 84, 86, 87, 107, 108-109, 112, 113, 115, 119, 122, 124, 125; Rodrigo Ramos: 94, 69; Alberto Rocha: 58-59, 110; Lucas Parolin: cover, pages 16, 17, 30, 56, 57, 79, 88, 90-, 93, 96, 111, 121; Fares Maese: pages 18, 19, 20, 31, 39, 47 (top), 64, 106, 114, 116, 117, 118, 120, 123, ; Studio Hive: pages 16, 34 (bottom two); Chris Trevas: page 85
Editorial: Delia Greve
Design: Sam Dawson
Production: Tom Miller

Printed, manufactured, and assembled in Shenzhen, China, 08/18

MIX
Paper from responsible sources
FSC® C017606

13803